Out of Retirement

By

Erica Lawson

Affinity
eBook Press
NZ
2014

Out of Retirement
© Erica Lawson 2014

Affinity E-Book Press NZ LTD.
Canterbury, New Zealand

1st Edition

ISBN: 978-1-927282-58-8

Editor: Nat Burns
Cover Design: Irish Dragon Designs

Acknowledgements

First, and foremost, I'd like to thank Affinity eBooks for the opportunity to publish this story, Julie, Erin and Nancy have gone beyond the call of duty with their authors and I commend them for their care.

I'd like to thank Mary for looking over the story for me and making sure I didn't have Mel and Caitlin kissing before they'd even met. Can't have that happen!

And the wonderful cover by Nancy K. Thank you.

A story can't be complete without an editor, and I had a good one. Thank you Nat Burns for sharing your expertise with me and I hope it shows in this book.

By Erica Lawson

Miss-Match with A. C. Henley

The Chronicles of Ratha: Children of the Noorthi

Possessing Morgan

Soulwalker

Reflected Passion

Dedication

All of us have, at one time or another, been touched by someone with Alzheimer's Disease. It reaches out to us in oh so many ways and shows us how fragile our memories can be. In the book one of the characters is said to have Alzheimer's. This is assumed by the characters. There has been no investigations done, nor does there seem to be any loss of short-term memory. She appears to be a sweet soul who lives in her memories. Let us hope that if it ever happens to us, we can show the world the best inside us.

Table of Contents

Chapter One

Into the Nuthouse

Melanie drove into the cracked, pocked driveway and parked her car behind a yellow Chevy station wagon that was easily ten years old and looked remarkably shabby. She got out, grabbed her bag and locked her car.

The house she had been called to showed signs of neglect. The peeling paint and the rusted gutters told a sad tale about the single story building. On the wall near the front door was a sign.

Shady Oakes had been spelled out in large letters, with Retirement Home added in smaller letters underneath. What drew Mel's attention was the removal of some of the letters, leaving behind a dirty outline of what had been there before. The remaining letters had been painted in bright red to highlight them. The sign now said Dykes Retirement Home.

"Okay," Mel said to herself.

Something hit her in the back and she turned to see a boy straddling a bike. At her feet lay a rolled-up newspaper.

"Come back here, you little runt!"

An old lady, barely five feet tall, jumped out of the bushes and ran toward the boy on the bike as fast as her elderly legs would carry her. She flailed a cane above her head and took a swipe or two in his direction.

The boy's eyes widened and he put his feet on the pedals. He pumped as hard as he could, to little effect. The bike responded slowly and finally broke away from whatever invisible force had held it in place.

"Crazy old woman!" he yelled.

"You tell them that we won't fall for their games. They want a fight, then come and get us!" She shook her fist at the departing boy then stomped down the driveway and up the small ramp to the

1

front door. She sniffed at Mel, opened the door, walked through and slammed it shut.

Mel blinked. Her mouth moved but nothing happened, so she blinked again. "Okay."

As her mind digested what had just happened, her hand rose and knocked on the door. It took a few seconds before she could hear movement on the other side.

"Isabel, could you see that Alice finds the right bed this time."

The door opened and a young woman stood there. Mel would have classed her as hot, but she tried not to react to her. Just because the sign said dykes didn't necessarily mean that everyone who lived in the house were so minded. Mel blinked again.

"Can I help you?" The woman's voice was low and husky.

"Errr." Mel's mouth opened and closed like a guppy and her finger pointed backward and forward from the road to the house. "I… I'm Dr. Stokes."

"Great!" The woman grabbed her hand and shook it enthusiastically.

"That woman…."

"Alice? She thinks she's in the Resistance. I'm surprised she didn't try to capture you."

"Capture me? She does this sort of thing often?" Mel tried to remember what she had learned about Alzheimer's.

"From time to time. She's getting on."

"I can see that. May I come in?"

It was obvious to Mel that the woman didn't realize she had left her standing on the doorstep for some time.

"Where are my manners? Come in, come in." She ushered Mel quickly into the room, as if she was expecting her to make a sudden escape. "I'm Caitlin, by the way."

"Nice to meet you, Caitlin. I'm Melanie, but most people call me Mel." Mel put down her bag. "Now, what seems to be the problem?"

"One of my girls said she needed some help."

"Help? What sort of help?"

"Why don't I let her tell you herself?"

Mel wondered what could be so awful that Caitlin couldn't say. She picked up her bag. "Lead on."

Mel checked out the house as she wandered through it. While the structure was a little run down, the inside had been kept immaculate. She revised her initial opinion about the state of disrepair. It was obviously a matter of money and not of care. Unfortunately, she had seen too many houses of late in the same condition.

"How many residents are there?"

"Residents?" Caitlin chuckled.

"Did I say something funny?"

"It sounds a lot better than patients or inmates." Caitlin entered the last room on the left.

"Sophie, the doctor's here! Now you behave yourself."

"Woo hoo, a lady doctor!" Sophie gave a loud wolf whistle and grinned.

Mel glanced at Caitlin, who shrugged her shoulders.

"So, Sophie. What seems to be the problem?" Mel placed her bag on the bed.

"Well, right now it's that I'm forty years too old, sugar." She winked at Mel, who blushed.

"She's got asteroids!" The miniature woman who had slammed the door in her face appeared in the doorway.

"Asteroids?"

"Hemorrhoids," Caitlin murmured.

"Ahh." Mel couldn't stop a chuckle as an image of two hemorrhoids shooting across the night sky like blazing comets came to mind. She glanced at Caitlin again.

"My girls are a little… feisty."

"Feisty? Really?"

"Do you think you can handle me, sugar?"

"It depends on what I'm handling you for." Mel brought her hands together to warm them, while Sophie laughed.

"Touché, sugar."

"You can call me Dr. Stokes." Mel tried to sound stern but she was sure Sophie would have none of it.

"Is she a Nazi spy?" Alice asked.

"No, she's here to help us," Caitlin responded

"Good, a Yankee paratrooper. Do you know field first aid?" Alice sidled up to Mel. "Let's see your I.D."

Mel reached into her bag and pulled out her driver's license. "Is that good enough?"

"All correct, Captain." Alice saluted Caitlin.

"Alice, go back to bed," Caitlin ordered, "and Sophie, no more nonsense. The doctor is a busy woman."

"She can be busy with me any time." Sophie gave a throaty laugh that sounded like she was choking. The laugh ended with a cough.

"Sophie!" A fifth voice entered the conversation.

"Phyllis, what are you doing here?"

"I heard a wolf whistle. I came to see what all the noise was about." Phyllis turned her gaze to Mel and gave her the once over. "New doc? I approve." She addressed Sophie, "Listen, my girl, you be nice around the doc. We can't afford to lose another one."

"Another one?" Mel took a mental step back.

"Sophie's a bit of a tease."

"No, really?" Mel couldn't keep the sarcasm out of her voice. "Then the sign on the building is not a joke."

"Not for me, darlin'." Sophie winked at Mel.

"Oh, Lord," Caitlin whispered.

"And how old are you, Sophie?"

"Seventy-seven years young. And you?"

"Sophie!"

"No, that's okay. I'm thirty-four."

"So, there's some hope for me yet."

"Maybe." Mel winked at Sophie. "I'm currently unattached."

"And what were you attached to?" Sophie continued.

"That's enough!" Phyllis moved into the room and used her wheelchair to clear the space she needed. "Don't answer that, Doc. It's none of her business."

"I have a feeling it's going to be a long debate in this house so I'll put you out of your misery. I like my attachments with skirts. But that information is top secret, okay?"

4

"Woo hoo! Hot diggety!" Sophie clapped.

"You shouldn't have said that," Phyllis warned.

"Why?"

"Because Sophie will make our lives miserable. She now thinks she's got a chance."

"What the hell are you talking about? Our love was made in heaven." Sophie reached for her shirt. "Unless you all want to cop an eyeful, I suggest you leave while the doc here examines me."

"There's no need to remove your blouse."

"But, where's the fun in that?" Sophie batted her eyelashes at Mel.

"Do you want me to stay?" Caitlin asked.

"Help," Mel cried quietly.

†

"I suppose it's too late to say I'm off the market," Mel said hopefully.

"It's all my fault." Caitlin said as she escorted Mel to the kitchen. "Have a cup of coffee before you go. You look like you need it."

Mel sat down at the kitchen table. She was numb. She'd never come across anyone quite like Sophie, young or old. A couple of minutes later a mug of steaming coffee sat in front of her. "Thanks."

"I don't know what to say. 'Sorry' is a good start, I suppose." Caitlin sat down opposite Mel with her own coffee in hand.

"No, it was my fault for playing her game." Mel took a sip of her coffee and stared out into space. "What do I do now?"

"The only thing to do is to get someone else to take your place for these visits. Trying to get a female doctor has been hard, especially from the Community Center."

"The ladies don't like men." It was a statement rather than a question for Mel.

"Not really, no. They tolerate them when they're sick."

"That doesn't leave me with a lot of choice then. I suppose I'll be your doctor until someone more suitable comes along."

"More suitable?" Caitlin tilted her head.

"You know, attached. Off the market. In a relationship. Straight."

"I get it. I suppose you could wait a few weeks then tell her you've got a girlfriend."

"And have Sophie try to string me up? Are you joking? Besides, she won't believe that."

"She doesn't know where you live." Caitlin chuckled.

"True, but unless I can produce the girlfriend I don't think she's going to believe me."

Caitlin stood up and went to the shelf and returned with a cookie jar. "Cookie?"

Mel felt her stomach rumble and decided that missing breakfast was not a good idea. "Thanks." She reached in and pulled out an oatmeal cookie.

"Don't worry. It's not like she's going to stalk you or anything."

"Stalk?" Mel's eyes grew wide. "How mobile is she?" She looked over her shoulder at the corridor. "I wonder if I can plant a GPS tracker on her."

"A tracker? The woman is seventy-seven years old."

"Seventy-seven, going on twenty-three." Mel took a huge mouthful of coffee and swirled it around in her mouth while she thought. After she swallowed, she spoke, "When does a woman's sex drive run out? I'll have to look it up back at the center."

"By the way Sophie is acting, I'd say she's had her tank re-filled." Caitlin smiled. "I'm sorry, but this is just too funny."

"Funny?" Mel looked at Caitlin. "You must be the only one. I'm terrified." Mel looked down at her hands and saw they were shaking.

Caitlin reached across the table and took her hand. "Stop worrying. It's one little old woman."

Mel looked at Caitlin's hand lying on her own. Quickly, she withdrew it. "Um, I better go."

"So soon? Oh, okay." Caitlin stood. "Thanks again for coming so quickly." Caitlin extended her hand and Mel took it, shaking it slowly and deliberately. "Let's hope Sophie suffers a bout of amnesia sometime soon."

"That would only make my job harder. As a doctor, I mean. However, my female persona will be cheering you on."

Caitlin escorted Mel to the front door and opened it to let Mel step out into the sunshine.

"I'll be in touch," Mel said.

"Fine." Caitlin looked at Mel. "Well, goodbye."

"Bye," Mel watched the door close. She stood there for a moment to allow the heat of the sun to seep into her body. In a way, it made her feel better, but she wasn't sure whether it was the weather or the fact that she was leaving the nuthouse.

Chapter Two

A New Game Plan

Caitlin closed the door and growled.

"Sophie!" She walked purposefully along the corridor to Sophie's room. "That was not funny, old woman!"

"Wasn't she a doll?"

"Do you know how hard it is to get a doctor to come here, let alone a female one?"

"Then you hit pay dirt. A female lesbian doctor. That's got to be a home run." Sophie giggled.

Caitlin looked at Phyllis, who shrugged her shoulders and shook her head.

"You leave her alone, you hear me? She's ready to run because of you."

"I'm just having some fun."

"No… more… fun." Caitlin pointed her finger at Sophie.

Sophie crossed her heart with her hand and held it up, swearing a silent oath.

Caitlin left the room and returned to the kitchen. "Why don't I feel like I'm in control?" But she knew why. Her small band of old women had very little to do except make her life a misery. She was used to it, but any stranger brave enough to visit didn't have her insight and took everything at face value. Now it looked like she was going to lose another doctor because Sophie couldn't keep her mouth shut.

Caitlin moved around the kitchen with ease. The local butcher had kindly donated a brisket to her cause and she busily prepared it for the oven. She hated taking handouts, but times were tough. Their combined income barely covered the bills and what was left Caitlin gave to her charges to buy luxuries to make life a little easier. She couldn't remember the last time she'd had money to spend on herself. Not that she minded. Her little band of warriors certainly made life interesting.

A high-pitched yell made Caitlin drop what she was doing and run out of the kitchen and down the corridor.

"What? What's wrong?" Her heart beat at a blistering pace. "Who died?"

Phyllis sat in her chair with a towel around her shoulders. "What the *hell* were you thinking?"

Isabel stood there blinking rapidly.

"I said *black* hair dye! What is this crap? How many times have I told you to take your glasses with you when you go shopping?"

"Hey!" Caitlin called but she went unnoticed.

"What am I supposed to do now?"

"What's going on?" Caitlin persisted.

"I thought it was the right hair dye. I'm sorry—" Isabel was crestfallen.

"Sorry won't cut it. I'm stuck with this now." Phyllis swung her wheelchair around and headed out of Isabel's room. "Jeezus, ask for one simple thing and all I get is grief."

Isabel stood there, her bottom lip quivering.

"Come on, now," Caitlin said while rubbing Isabel's back. "She didn't mean it. She'll get over it soon enough."

"I didn't take my glasses."

"I should have checked it for you. After all, I was with you when you bought it."

"Then it's your fault." Isabel said cheerfully. She seemed satisfied she had passed on the blame and shuffled out of the room. "It's Caitlin's fault!" she yelled. "She just admitted it!"

Why didn't she see that one coming? However, Phyllis was now stuck with pink hair until the next social security check arrived. Phyllis would not be a happy camper.

Caitlin returned to the kitchen and put the brisket in the oven, turning the temperature down low to allow the meat to cook gently. She refilled her mug and sat at the table to savor a moment's silence. There were other chores to do, but somehow she couldn't summon up the enthusiasm to do any of them.

"C'mon, Cait, old girl. They won't get done by themselves." When she couldn't put it off any longer, Caitlin washed her mug and went in search of the laundry.

She collected the dirty clothes and put them into one pile. This ritual had been done often enough that she knew all the clothes intimately, so the time had long passed since she had given Phyllis's underpants to Sophie. It was an expensive mistake to rectify because Phyllis refused to wear them ever again. Now she knew them by size, from teenage girl to circus tent. Besides, she had meticulously written their names in each piece to ensure the same mistake never happened again—at least not accidentally.

Phyllis rolled by in her wheelchair.

"Hey," Caitlin called.

"Yeah?" Phyllis said grumpily.

"Don't take it out on Isabel. I should have checked it before she bought it."

"Awww, hell! I can't be mad at you."

"Pink, huh?"

"I could have put up with gray or even blue, but pink! Good Lord, Caitlin, a dyke with pink hair. That's just inhumane!"

"Next check we'll fix it up, okay?"

"We can't do anything about it now?"

"Sorry, I'm all out of spare cash. The rest is already spoken for."

"Look," Phyllis rolled her wheelchair closer, "we all appreciate what you do for us. Don't ever doubt that. We know it can't be easy for you. When was the last time you went out on a date?"

"A date? What's that?" Caitlin laughed. "Don't you worry about it. I'm happy with things the way they are…for now."

"You're not getting any younger, my girl."

"I'm only twenty-eight. I'm not over the hill yet."

"These should be the best years of your life, but you're stuck here looking after us. Just because Ellen…."

"It was my decision, Phyllis. Grandma loved this place and I do too. If I can make it a little easier for you girls…." Phyllis reached out and patted Caitlin's hand. "Now let me get back to the laundry."

"I'll be out the front if you need me."

"Don't go too far," Caitlin said, but she had already turned back to the washing.

Caitlin carried out the first basket laden with wet clothes. She returned to the house to get the hangers and clothespins. On the spur of the moment she detoured to Alice's room. "Hey, Alice! Do you want to help me on a mission?"

"A mission?" Alice looked up from her book. The rather ratty-looking novel had been read many, many times.

"Aren't you sick of reading that yet?"

"This? I haven't read this before. Why?"

"Nothing." That was the wonderful thing about dementia; a few minutes later everything was new again.

Alice put down her copy of "The Diary of Anne Frank" and followed Caitlin outside.

"Okay, Alice, your mission is to get six potatoes, four carrots and a handful of beans from the vegetable garden. Have you got that? Six potatoes, four carrots, and a handful of beans, nothing more."

"I'm not stupid. I've got that. However, I wouldn't stand around here if I were you. There are snipers everywhere." Alice walked off and did a wide loop around the backyard. When she got close enough to the garden she dropped to the ground and began to crawl.

"What are you doing? Get up!"

"Shhhh. They'll hear you! You're a sitting target." Alice waved her hands in an effort to get Caitlin to drop to the ground as well.

Caitlin kept an eye on her and, despite her age, Alice seemed unconcerned that she was on her hands and knees. Caitlin watched her crawl to, and over, the garden to retrieve her booty. "There goes another outfit."

11

Alice dug with her hands, pulling out the potatoes and carrots with enthusiasm. "Mission accomplished, Captain."

"Alice!" A second later Caitlin was next to her. "Stand up. Your knees can't take this."

Alice grabbed her and pulled her to the dirt. "Careful, the enemy is everywhere."

When it looked like Alice wasn't going anywhere until Caitlin complied, she dropped to the ground. "Right. Come on, let's go."

Alice turned around and crawled back across the garden, leaving flattened carrots tops and potato greenery in her wake.

Caitlin rolled her eyes, but duck-waddled behind her to keep the old woman happy. Once they were clear of the war zone, Caitlin stood up and helped Alice to her feet. "Good work, corporal. Now return the goods to the kitchen and I will see to your reward." She dusted the dirt of Alice.

Alice smiled. It was a small thing, but her praise, and her willing participation of the charade, had its rewards.

Alice trotted back in the house while Caitlin turned to hang out the washing. The sun was out and there was a gentle breeze. It was another nice day. "The beans." Caitlin walked to the garden and picked her handful of beans for dinner. "She nearly got it right." Maybe one day Alice would remember everything.

There was a brief scream and Caitlin moved quickly to find the source of the sound. "Now what?"

Chapter Three

Flying By the Seat of Her Pants

Phyllis parked her wheelchair on the sidewalk near the front gate of her home. She was still fuming about the mix-up of the hair dye, but there was nothing that could be done. Whether she liked it or not, she was stuck with pink hair.

The anger bled from her slowly. While she could blame Isabel for her dilemma, or even to a lesser extent Caitlin, she could also blame herself for not noticing the difference before she applied it to her hair.

She sat there for half an hour and watched the world go by. The sun was out and the heat beat down on her. If she didn't go inside soon her hair would frizz and she'd look like a circus clown.

"Fuck!" she spat out. She was an old woman and it depressed her. Her life had been lived and now it was all downhill. It had hurt to give up her beloved bike all those years ago, but her last accident made sure she'd never ride again. It was like losing a part of her soul, because that bike had been at the center of her identity. "A dyke on a bike", she muttered. That phrase conjured up images of long highways, life-long friendships and easy loving. It was a time in her life that made all the bad times fade away. But time, like her life, had now passed and she was left with the faded memories of her wild days.

While Phyllis's mind played back her hell-on-wheels days, she absently watched a small removal van drive by. There was nothing special about it. It was a white enclosed van with Parker's Removals emblazoned on the side. What she hadn't noticed was the length of rope trailing along behind it; at least not until a second before it wound its way around the bottom of her wheelchair.

Phyllis felt the tug a second before the rope drew taut. The brake lever snapped off and skittered into the gutter. She set off with a jerk and barreled down the road after the van. Phyllis let out a brief scream, but the bumpy ride knocked the breath out of her. With no other option, she sat back, held on tight and closed her eyes. The memories in her head swirled around, accentuated by the wind on her face and the feeling of speed underneath her. It was like stepping back in time… and she adored it.

"Woo hoo!" she cried. When her body caught up to the speed she was doing she opened her eyes and smiled. "Fuckin' awesome!" Phyllis knew she could get away with saying those words, at least for now. Caitlin didn't like cussing in the house. It was then that she saw the van's indicator light go on and they were about to make a turn. "Oh, crap…."

†

Mel's vehicle turned the last corner and onto the street where Caitlin and her wily old band of lesbians were living. It was then that she spotted the van and its unwilling captive trailing behind.

"Oh, shit!" She put her foot down and caught up with the van. She blasted her horn, but the driver didn't slow down. He stuck his hand out the window and waved her on.

Mel sped up until she was level with the cabin and wildly pointed to the back of his van. The kid inside cupped his hand to his ear and shook his head. Short of cutting him off, he wasn't going to stop. She was nearly going to do that, but realized the sudden stop could be fatal for the reluctant passenger in tow.

"Slow down!" she yelled. Mel pressed the window button and yelled again. "Slow down! You've got an old woman caught up on the back of your van!"

The kid grinned. He sped on, obviously not believing what she said. He turned left at the next corner and Mel watched in horror as Phyllis's wheelchair sped by before swinging in a wide arc.

"Oh, God!" Mel slammed on the brakes hard and waited for Phyllis to land. She flew into the air when the chair hit the curb, and gracefully flipped to land in the front yard of someone's home. She came to an abrupt stop on a pile of autumn leaves.

"Hey, jerk! You just killed her!" Mel screamed. The van came to a screeching halt and the kid jumped out.

"Holy shit! You weren't kidding!" He ran to Phyllis and looked down at her. "Do something!"

Mel grabbed her bag and ran to an immobile Phyllis. Her immediate impression was that Phyllis was dead. While there seemed to be no visible signs of trauma, besides a scratch here and there, she knew only too well that much more serious injuries could lie underneath, especially in kids and the elderly.

Phyllis opened her eyes and looked up. "Hi there, Doc," she said, almost too cheerfully. "Can we do that again?"

"What the hell were you doing?"

"I didn't *do* anything. It just happened." Phyllis's eyebrows met in an angry V. "Blame this guy." She pointed at the young man standing by nervously. "If he'd tied off his rope properly this wouldn't have happened." Phyllis tried to lift herself.

"Don't move. Something could be broken." Mel rested her hand on Phyllis's shoulder.

"I'd know if something was broken by now." Phyllis was miffed. "Now, get out of my way."

"Hey! I'm the doctor here and I say you stay put." Mel reached into her bag and took out her cell.

"I don't need a damned ambulance."

"Since when did you graduate medical school?" Mel punched in 911 and waited for the operator.

"Before you were born, missy. Hang up."

"At your age—"

"At my age, Doc, I think I know if I'm injured or not." She neglected to mention the pain in her left middle finger because she knew it would mean instant transport to the hospital.

"Please, for my peace of mind, at least get checked out. Just a few hours for X-rays, okay?"

Phyllis knew it was a big concession on the doc's part and, as much as she wanted to tell her to forget it, she reluctantly agreed.

15

"Take a picture," Phyllis muttered.

Mel looked at her phone then at Phyllis. "Why? Is this for the cover of *Biker's Monthly* or *Harper's Bazaar*?"

"A picture of the wheelchair," Phyllis ground out.

"For crying out loud, woman, you're injured."

Caitlin ran up to the scene. "Holy hell! What happened?"

"Phyllis couldn't wait to climb back into the saddle."

"Is she okay? Are you okay?" Caitlin moved restlessly in the one spot.

"I'm fine," Phyllis said. "Come here." She beckoned Caitlin, who walked to her and crouched down. "I can't seem to get it into this woman's head that we need pictures of the crime scene."

"What on earth for?"

Phyllis looked at the kid pacing near his van, speaking urgently into his cell. Phyllis grabbed Caitlin's lapels and pulled her down to within inches from her face. "In case they decide to skip out on paying for the damage. Jeez, can't anyone think?"

"Unlike you, we are more worried about you than your chair." Mel said.

"Worrying about me ain't gonna pay the bills, Doc. Please, just do it."

"I'm looking after you."

"Then... give... the... goddamned... phone... to... Caitlin. Do I have to do everything around here?"

Mel did as she was ordered. "Is she always this bossy?"

Caitlin nodded and began to take pictures of the scene. "I feel like CSI."

"A dime store version of it," Phyllis grumbled. "Now, get me back into my chair."

"I hate to tell you, honey, but your chair is all banged up."

"You want me to sit on the ground?"

"Is that a problem?" Mel asked. "You can lie down if you want."

"How many times do I have to say there's nothing wrong with me?"

"As many times as you like. Until the EMTs are here you are not moving."

Phyllis glared at Mel, who glared back at her. She was damned if some chick doctor was going to tell her what to do. Phyllis growled and pointed her finger at Mel. "You are in deep trouble, missy."

"Yeah, yeah. Join the line." Mel started to walk toward Caitlin, who was happily snapping pictures of the crime scene, before she turned and ordered, "Stay put!"

"No one's ever told me what to do."

"There's always a first."

Before Phyllis could comment Mel had moved away. Who the hell did she think she was? Just then she heard the sound of a siren. "You've won this round, Doc." She wasn't quite sure whether that was a threat or a promise. Time would tell.

Chapter Four

Doctor One, Patient Nil

"You have got to be the luckiest woman alive." That was all Mel could say. Phyllis sat up in bed and regaled her adventure to the others. Phyllis went to the hospital for cursory a checkup then insisted on coming home. While Mel wasn't happy with the arrangement, to allay her own fears she decided to stick around the retirement home to keep an eye on Phyllis herself. She was quite amused that Phyllis's broken finger had been splinted by an intern who didn't seem to care that his work had left her 'giving the finger' to one and all. When she offered to fix it, Phyllis declined. She rather liked the idea of the visual statement.

"It was amazing, Doc. Took me back to the old days."

"Old days?"

"Oh, yeah. Phyll here is a rebel. She was at Stonewall." Mel could hear the pride in Sophie's voice as she spoke of that event. "Tell her, Phyll. Tell her about Stonewall."

"Not much to tell. I was there." However, Phyllis's body language told another story. She didn't want to talk about it.

"Come on, then. She needs her rest." Mel ushered everyone out and gave Phyllis one final look before she closed the door.

"It sure was lucky you were in the neighborhood," Caitlin said. "So why were you in the neighborhood?"

"I was nearly back at the Community Center when I realized I hadn't given you a script for Sophie. I was on my way back here when I saw Miss Stonewall heading off down the street."

"Not that she needed your help. Phyllis was ready to interrogate the poor boy."

"It was pretty sloppy work on his part. He should have secured that rope."

"Maybe he had and it worked itself loose. Accidents happen."

"It sounds like this is Accident Central. Maybe I should open a branch here and save on time and gas."

"Sure. I could rent out one of the back rooms." Caitlin said, "You could hang your shingle out front."

"Ha ha." Mel followed Caitlin into the kitchen and sat down at the table. Caitlin automatically found the mugs and made more coffee. "I'll be sticking around here for a while to make sure there aren't any complications from the crash."

"We're only having brisket, but you're welcome to stay for dinner."

Mel sniffed the air. "If that's only brisket, it smells pretty good. I'd love to stay." Mel took notice when Caitlin smiled. "Can I pick up something for dinner? Drink perhaps?"

"We don't normally have alcohol, but don't let me stop you if you want something. There's a liquor store a couple of blocks away."

"Maybe later." Mel settled back in the chair and sighed. "Are things always this chaotic around here?"

"They can be, although I think today is in honor of your arrival."

"Now I feel special."

"Really? I'm sure the ladies can think up some more things for you to do."

"No! No!" Mel waved her free hand. "That's fine." Caitlin laughed at her. "Is this how you welcome all your guests?"

"Only the special ones."

"Well, I think you deserve a medal."

"Ahh, no I don't. It has its own rewards."

Mel put down her mug. "Speaking of rewards, how long has it been since you've had a break?"

"I don't mind."

"That long, huh? Well, prepare yourself for the movies tonight."

"What about the ladies?"

"I'll take care of that." Mel reached into her pocket. "Excuse me for a minute. I'll just make a call."

Caitlin watched Mel leave the kitchen and heard the front door open and close a moment later. She was going on a date. When she couldn't hold it in any longer, she punched the air. "Yesssssssss."

"Yes?" Mel stood in the doorway slightly amused.

"Err, yes. I just checked the roast and everything is fine."

"Fine. Riiightt." Mel sat down on the chair. "I've got tonight covered."

"That's good to hear."

"I suppose now is a good time to get to know the ladies. Do you happen to know what medications all your residents are taking? It might be of help in the future."

Caitlin walked to a clipboard hanging on the side of a cupboard and brought it to the table. "Here you go. A list of medications for each resident."

"Four? Is that all you have?"

"For now. I had a couple of extra ladies six months ago, but when their families realized what sort of place this was, they withdrew them immediately."

"This place?"

"Lesbians," Caitlin mouthed.

"Oh. It's their loss."

"And mine," Caitlin said wistfully.

Mel reached into her bag and pulled out her prescription pad. "This should do the trick for Sophie." She wrote quickly and referred to Caitlin's paperwork for a name and address. "If you have any further problems...," Mel reached into her pocket and withdrew a business card, "...give me a call. My private number is on the back." She scrawled her number on the card. Mel watched Caitlin attach the card and the script to her clipboard.

"What can you tell me about them?"

Caitlin walked to the shelf and got down the cookie jar. "When did you last eat?"

"The last thing I ate was the cookie you gave me this morning. Are you trying to fatten me up?"

"Sorry, it's a habit."

"So I'm more a septuagenarian in your eyes." Mel grinned at Caitlin's obvious fluster.

"No! Whatever gave you that idea?"

"Because you're treating me like one of your residents."

"Is that a bad thing?"

"No, but I had hoped I made more of an impression than an old lady."

"Old *lesbian* lady," Caitlin corrected.

"But still an old lady, I see." Mel's grin dissolved into a laugh.

"I didn't... don't...mean...."

"Don't worry about it."

"Another coffee?"

Mel smiled wryly.

"I'm doing it again, aren't I?"

"What are you so nervous about? I'm not going to eat you."

Caitlin turned away and filled the kettle. She placed it on the stove and collected the two mugs.

"What can you tell me about Sophie?"

"Sophie?"

"Her background."

"Sophie's seventy-seven."

"I know that. She made a point of telling me." Mel felt a shiver run down her spine and Caitlin laughed.

"Her husband died about twenty years ago. It was then that she discovered she was a lesbian."

"She was married... to a man?"

"No to an orangutan. Of course, a man!"

"Has she always been so..."

"Promiscuous?" Caitlin supplied.

"I was thinking more forward, but promiscuous works."

"From what she said the marriage was okay. They had a child but he died at age twenty from some sort of disease. The marriage lost its appeal after that. It was like the son held the family together. When he died so did the love."

"Why didn't she just divorce him?"

"She had nowhere else to go. She was happy to leave things be. A few years after that, her husband died of a heart attack."

"And she decided she was a lesbian."

"That's what she said. She came into my care about five years ago when she could no longer afford regular nursing home care."

"Ahh, now I get it. You collect waifs."

"No, I… well I suppose you could call it that."

"What about Alice? She's got to be a handful."

"Not a lot is known about Alice. As you can see, she lives in her own little world, so anything she says has to be taken with a grain of salt."

"How long has she been here?"

"Going on ten years. My grandmother took her in when the hospital was about to turn her back out onto the street."

"What did your grandmother do? Troll the hospitals for likely candidates?"

"No, she just happened to be in the right place at the right time."

"You know, the average person on the street would say she was in the wrong place at the wrong time."

"And I would have missed out on the most wonderful glimpses of a mind full of curiosity and joy."

"Did you ever find out why she focuses on the Resistance?"

"I have no idea. Maybe one day she'll reveal it to me. Of course, she reads "The Diary of Anne Frank" all the time. For now, we play games to keep her amused and out of trouble."

"Aren't you scared of her walking out one day and never coming back?"

"It's really strange."

"You can say that again."

"It's really strange, but she seems to know this is her home, although she has done some really weird things in the last few years."

"Yeah? Like what?"

"About six months ago she tunneled under the side fence and captured the dog next door to interrogate him as a Nazi collaborator."

"How far did she get?"

"Let's just say the dog hasn't walked the same since."

"Isabel."

"Isabel. She's a spinster. It's probably because she's so shy, even though she does have her moments."

"How do you know she's a lesbian? She told you?"

"Not in so many words."

"So, a lesbian by omission. Interesting."

"Not everyone has to shout it out to the world."

"Like me, you mean?" Mel's eyebrow shot up.

"You didn't have to tell Sophie."

"I suppose I didn't. I was trying to get a rapport going."

"Instead you got a date."

"How was I to know she wanted to screw anything that moved?"

"Now you know."

"Now I know. All right, that takes care of Isabel. Now the big one. Phyllis. There was mention of Stonewall and she went quiet. What happened?"

"All I ever heard her say was that she was there. Sophie's the one who gets all excited about it. Phyllis had a rough childhood. Her parents threw her out of the house at fourteen when she came out. I'm not sure what happened for the next ten years or so, but something happened to turn her life around. She managed to hold down the odd job or two for a few years then she bought herself a bike and wandered the highways for the next twenty years."

"A real dyke on a bike. I wanted to do that once. Leave my life behind me for a while."

"But you became a doctor."

"Yeah. From a biker to a doctor. My life took a wrong turn before I could buy that bike."

"Something happened," Caitlin said.

"Mom died. Dad didn't take it too well and I had to take care of him. He simply fell apart."

"And a doctor?"

"I suppose it was a natural progression from caregiver to doctor. I'd studied up enough to look after him, so I thought I might as well keep studying."

"And you have a successful practice."

"Yeah, but at the moment I'm doing volunteer work at the Community Center."

"Feeling a little guilty?"

"About what?"

"Doing volunteer work usually means there is some guilt involved."

Mel studied Caitlin, trying to decide whether she was being sarcastic or not. "No, no guilt that I know of. I'm just filling in while the regular doctor is on holiday. It's only a temporary thing." She waited while Caitlin made the coffee and brought it to the table. "Of course, if I hadn't been doing volunteer work I never would have met you."

"Me?" Caitlin squeaked.

"Yes, you. The home. Your little band of fiery feminists." Mel drank her coffee.

"Oh," Caitlin said, as if she had been let down.

"If you were offered more residents, would you take them?" Mel asked.

"I don't know. Why?"

"I have a patient at my practice who is looking for a placement. She lost her husband a year ago and now her home feels empty. Any objections to a straight woman?"

"I suppose not. Would she object? Then again, I don't know about my lot either."

"I could bring her for a day visit and see how they react to one another."

"You make her sound like a Labrador. Bring her over to see if she'll pee on the carpet or chew the furniture before giving her a home."

"I thought that was what Alice was for."

"One day I'll have to tell you about the time she tried jumping off the roof believing she was parachuting into Poland."

Mel sat up. "Holy... Did she break anything? Surely—"

"I managed to talk her down before she did any major damage, but she did a number on her right knee getting down the ladder. It's slowed her right down."

"Slowed her down? You mean she was quicker than she is now?" Caitlin nodded.

"She lost her balance halfway down and she fell into the garden. Squashed the gardenias flat. Before the accident she could out-sprint me—and she was seventy-five at the time."

"Thank God for small mercies."

"Thank God?"

"At least you can catch her now before she tries to invade Germany."

Caitlin just smiled.

"Oh no, she didn't?"

"Like I said, it's a story for another day." Caitlin sipped her coffee.

"And what about you? What's your story?"

"Nothing really to tell."

"You run a volunteer retirement home and there's not a story to tell? I beg to differ. There must be at least a mini-series or a movie of the week in it."

Caitlin smiled behind her mug. "My mom and dad died in a car accident. Grandma raised me and I took it on when it became too much for her. A couple of years later she passed and I've been running it ever since."

"How long ago was that?"

"Five years, give or take."

"You really do need a night off."

"It's been so long I don't even know what a night off is any more."

"Uh huh." Mel studied Caitlin with interest. "And that little 'yessss' I heard a while back? And don't tell me it was the roast because I don't believe it for one minute."

"All right. You caught me. I'm rather looking forward to tonight."

"That's good to hear. Be ready by seven-thirty." Mel finished up her coffee and stood. "Now I better go and check on my patient. After all, that's what I'm here for.

Chapter Five

Into The Lion's Den

Mel left Caitlin in the kitchen and walked down the hallway to Phyllis's room. She found her sitting up in bed looking out the window. "Everything okay?"

Phyllis turned her attention to Mel. "Fine."

"You look a little pensive there."

"Just thinking."

Mel smiled. She didn't want to point out that 'pensive' and 'thinking' meant the same thing. Some things were universal, and embarrassment was near the top of the list. Mel delved into her bag and pulled out her stethoscope.

"Again? Can't we skip it this time?" Phyllis whined. "I'm fine. Really."

Mel moved walked across the room and pulled up a chair. "What's wrong?"

"And you call yourself a doctor." Phyllis huffed.

"I am for the physical stuff; not so much for the emotional stuff."

"Are you trying to say that I'm nuts?" Phyllis said.

"Are you always on the defensive?" Mel responded.

"When it comes to my mental state, you betcha."

"I just thought you might like to talk about it."

"It? I thought you being an 'out and about' lesbian would know all about 'it'. In fact, you could probably teach me a new thing or two."

Mel laughed. "I don't think so, but a biker gal like you has probably done things I've only dreamed about."

"I doubt it."

Mel bit the bullet. "About Stonewall."

"There's nothing to tell. I was there."

"So you said," Mel said, "but surely being such a historic moment there must be more to it than that."

"And being such a historic moment," Phyllis ground out, "it has been well documented and does not need my input."

"So that's it, huh?"

"That's it."

"That's disappointing. Maybe I should ask Sophie about it. She seems more enthusiastic about it than you are."

"Maybe you should." Phyllis turned her gaze to the window.

"Dinner will be in a couple of hours. Do you feel like getting up for it?"

"That depends on you."

Mel grew tired of Phyllis's hostility. "I leave the decision up to you. Don't answer now. I'm sure Caitlin will be by soon and you can tell her then."

Mel stood and placed the chair against the wall. Without a word she left the room. Half way down the corridor she muttered, "Bitch."

"I heard that!" Phyllis yelled.

†

Dinner was eaten in companionable silence. Alice devoured hers like she was on a deadline, while Phyllis pushed her food around the plate. Mel looked at Caitlin, who shook her head.

"Thank you for the drink," Caitlin said brightly. "I can't remember the last time I had wine."

"I hope chardonnay was fine. I know its red wine with meat, but I'm not a red drinker."

"Anything with alcohol in it is fine with me," Sophie added.

"Yeah, thanks," Phyllis said sullenly. She lifted her glass of beer and took a mouthful. Once she had swallowed, her tongue emerged to wipe the froth from her lips. "Been a while."

"That blows this month's rations," Alice added as she drank her wine. "Where did you get it, Major? This must be black market."

27

"I got it at the liquor... from the quartermaster. He owes me a favor or two."

"Ahh. Well done." Alice settled back in her chair, glass in hand.

A quiet chuckle moved around the table and Mel glanced at Caitlin as she joined in. Mel gave her a smile.

"Captain, why are you wearing your dress uniform?"

Caitlin glanced down at her crisp white shirt and charcoal gray pants. "I'm going on a date."

"Really?" Phyllis asked and perked up. She studied Mel. "Where are you taking her?"

"Me? No, not me."

"You're not?" Caitlin looked crestfallen.

"I have a friend coming over and he's going to take you to the movies."

"Why not you?" Sophie asked.

"Someone has to stay here. I know you girls and he doesn't. It seemed the logical thing for me to stay. Right?"

"Right," Caitlin said flatly.

"Wrong," Isabel whispered.

"Sorry, did you say something?" Caitlin looked around the table. "What's wrong? I think it's a very generous offer."

"Yeah, sure." Phyllis cut up the meat and stuffed a piece in her mouth.

"But why a he?" Sophie asked.

"Alex was free tonight. Besides, I didn't want to assume that Caitlin was... you know."

"Yeah, I know—" Caitlin sighed.

"I don't. What is she talking about, Captain?"

"She's asking whether I'm a lesbian or not."

"You are? I don't know what to say."

"Alice, you're one too."

"I am? Why didn't someone tell me?"

"Because... oh, never mind." Phyllis returned to her meal.

"I'm a lesbian? How did that happen?"

"It's like this—" Sophie began.

"Don't! Just… don't." Phyllis held up her hand to stop any further comment. She directed her next question to Mel. "What's on for this evening then, Doc? Half an hour of TV, paddle our backsides and then off to bed?"

"Hot diggity! This evening is getting better by the minute!" Sophie clapped her hands with glee.

"You are such a horn dog!"

"And you are a wet blanket."

"Ladies! Please! Can we at least finish dinner?" Caitlin glanced at Mel. "Are you sure you want to do this?"

"What could possibly go wrong?" Mel offered. She didn't see Phyllis smile devilishly.

"You have just signed your own death warrant," Caitlin replied.

"What are you talking about?"

"You didn't cross your fingers behind your back or spit over your shoulder."

"Do you really do that?"

"Mentally, yes. You have now hexed yourself. And you said it in front of them." Caitlin glanced at each of the four women looking at her. "All I can say is… good luck."

"I have everything under control."

"If you say so." Caitlin returned to her meal and took the last bite. "Dessert anyone?"

†

"Have a great night!" Mel called from the doorway. She waved off Alex and Caitlin and watched them walk down the driveway to his car parked at the curb. She frowned momentarily when Alex's hand touched Caitlin's lower back to help her into the passenger seat.

"That's not good." Mel turned to find Phyllis behind her.

"What's not good?"

"He's making moves on her already." Phyllis glanced up at Mel before turning her wheelchair around.

Mel turned her gaze back to the car. It was still parked and she wondered what was going on inside. "But she's gay, right?"

"I don't know. She never actually said it."

Mel waited impatiently while Alex took his time starting up the car. She saw Caitlin laughing. "Damn," Mel muttered. "So," she closed the door and turned to find four women watching her, "what do you want to do now?" She tried to sound cheerful but for some reason she felt deflated.

"How about Scrabble®?"

"Sure, let's play Scrabble®." Phyllis said the words slowly and distinctly, giving Mel the impression she was about to descend into the depths of hell itself.

"You set up the board and I'll bring out the drinks." She disappeared into the kitchen and collected the spare beer and bottle of wine from the fridge. It was going to be a long night.

By the time she returned the board had been set up and the women were seated around the dining room table. A space had been left vacant for her, which seemed to put her in the middle of the group. They had her closed in from both sides.

"Everyone grab their tiles." Mel passed around the cans of beer and poured a wine for herself and Alice. The silence was broken by the clatter of tiles, arranged then re-arranged as each one tried to make sense of the jumble of letters they'd picked. "Who wants to go first?" There was silence. "Okay, then it's me." Mel studied the letters as she looked for a word. The grabbed the tiles and put them down on the board. "Your turn, Sophie." She picked up more tiles and added them to her rack.

"Melons?"

Sophie snickered.

"What's wrong with that?"

"Nothing," Phyllis said, "nothing at all."

Sophie continued to giggle as she put down her tiles.

"Lick. Are we keeping score?" Mel looked around for some paper.

"No, it's just for fun."

"Fine. Your turn, Isabel."

"My turn," Alice butted in, placing her tiles down before anyone could stop her. "There!"

"Sniper," Phyllis said. "Why am I not surprised?"

"Isabel?" Mel tried to keep the game moving. When Isabel lay her tiles down, Mel blushed. "Err, are we going to allow that?"

"What do you mean? It's a perfectly valid word." Phyllis looked at , shocked. "Doc, I'm surprised at you! Get that mind of yours out of the gutter!"

The letters on the board stood out and in Mel's mind were circled with flashing lights. "Prick?"

"You prick your finger, don't you?"

"Yes, but—"

"Then don't be a fuddy-duddy."

Mel laughed. She thought she'd be the one telling them that. "Your turn, Phyllis."

When Phyllis grinned at her wickedly, she had second thoughts. "Keep it clean."

"Whatever do you mean?" Phyllis's fingers hovered above the tiles.

"If you can't play properly I may reconsider the half hour of TV, a paddle on the behind and off to bed."

"You are such a tease," Sophie said seductively.

The tiles were slipped onto the board one by one, finally spelling out the word 'finger'.

"Do you want me to explain what that means?"

"Don't be a smart ass." Mel glared at Phyllis. "If you don't want to play, say so."

"I didn't say that."

"Then what are you saying, Phyllis? I don't know what I've done to piss you off. So unless you're going to tell me what's bothering you let's play this game amicably."

"You're the boss."

"No, I'm not. Caitlin is the boss. I'm here as your doctor, and hopefully as a friend."

"How about cards?" Alice suggested.

"Yeah, cards will be good," Isabel agreed.

Before Mel had a chance to give an opinion the tiles had been piled on the board. "So much for that game," she muttered.

Isabel disappeared into the kitchen and returned with a jar full of peas.

"What's that for?"

"You can't play poker without chips."

"Poker?" Mel held up her hands. "Now, hang on. I can't encourage gambling."

"Which is why we use peas. We can all afford these." Isabel unscrewed the lid and spilled the contents across the table. Phyllis, Sophie, Alice and Isabel scrambled to gather in the rolling peas, each making a pile in front of them.

"Oh boy."

✝

Mel woke with a start as the front door opened. "Hey," she called quietly, "how was the movie?"

"Fine."

But to Mel Caitlin didn't sound very enthusiastic. "What happened?" Had Alex overstepped his mark and made a move on Caitlin? "Everything all right?"

"Yeah. Just tired, I guess."

"I'm sorry if it wasn't what you wanted. I thought you could use a break."

"Don't apologize. It was very thoughtful and much appreciated."

"Come," Mel beckoned her to the sofa. "Sit. What's wrong?"

"Nothing really. I think Alex had the wrong idea about tonight."

"Do I need to have a word with him?"

"No, I set him straight."

Straight. It was a word that Mel hoped didn't apply to Caitlin. "About what?" she asked nervously.

"About being straight."

Hallelujah! Mel's insides jumped with giddy glee. "You mean, you're not…"

32

"Uh huh."

"So that sign on the door…."

"…is one hundred percent correct."

Mel tried very hard to keep her emotions from showing on her face.

"Would you like a coffee?" Caitlin stood up and moved to the kitchen.

"Do you think I'm a coffee junkie?"

Caitlin stuck her head out the door. "Why?"

"Every time I come within ten feet of you, you offer me coffee."

"Are you saying 'no'?"

"No. I'm just pointing out a fact."

"What did you do tonight?" Caitlin called from the kitchen.

"We played Scrabble®."

Caitlin returned to the sofa and sat on the armrest. "Oh."

"Yes, oh."

Caitlin reached down and picked up a pea off the floor. "And you played poker as well." She held the pea between her thumb and forefinger. "How much did you lose?"

"Two hundred and forty. You could have warned me. Alice played like some sort of demented Rainman."

"She counts the cards."

"Which is, as far as I know, illegal."

"What can I say? She has the knack."

"For a woman who is supposed to have Alzheimer's, Alice has an unerring ability to make the rest of us look like idiots."

"It's a gift." The kettle whistled and Caitlin returned to the kitchen. A minute later she returned with two mugs.

Mel recognized the mug. "Is this mug mine now?"

"I only have six. The odds were good you'd end up with the same one." She disappeared once more into the kitchen before returning with the cookie jar.

"You're trying to fatten me up." Mel said as Caitlin took a seat across the table.

"What's one cookie?"

"Not much, except when you multiply it by six cups of coffee each day."

"You exaggerate."

"Maybe." Despite her protest Mel took a sip from her mug.

"Tell me about this woman you want to bring."

"Her name is Doris Hansen. Sixty-nine years old and a widow. Her husband died about a year ago. Since then she's become more isolated."

"No children?"

"One daughter, but she only sees her occasionally."

"Maybe she needs to get out more. Make some friends."

"She tried that, but with not much success." Mel reached for the cookie jar. Caitlin's smirk did not go unseen. "It's your fault."

"You don't have to eat them."

"And you don't have to bring them out and leave them there to tempt me." Mel took a bite and munched for a moment. "Back to Doris. Sandra, her daughter, suggested a retirement home but she's a little reluctant to take that step."

"What do you think we can offer Doris?"

"You're a smaller group, mostly mobile and on the ball mentally."

"You flatter us," Caitlin said sarcastically.

"You know what I mean."

"No, I don't."

Mel pursed her lips. "I just thought I'd see if Doris was interested. If you don't want the business, that's fine by me."

"At present, four is about all I can manage. Besides, my car won't fit another one."

"What has your car got to do with it?"

"Sometimes I take them out on a day trip to get them out of the house."

"Oh, okay."

"All right. Bring her. Maybe she won't like it here."

"And if she does?"

"Let's worry about that bridge when we get to it."

"I haven't talked to Doris about this yet, but how about next Saturday, say 9 a.m.? I'll call you and let you know what's happening once I've talked to her." Mel stood and walked to the nightstand near the front door. She reached into her handbag and pulled out a business card and a pen. When she sat down again she handed the card to Caitlin. "Write your number on the back." Once Caitlin had complied Mel stood. "I really should get going. I've got an early appointment tomorrow. It won't do for the doctor to fall asleep during an examination."

Caitlin stood and walked with Mel to the door. "Thanks for tonight. You have no idea how much I appreciate it."

"My pleasure. I figured you needed a break, even if it was with a guy. Next time I'll arrange a woman."

"Good plan."

Mel claimed her bag and slipped the card and pen inside. She fished around for her keys. "So, I suppose I'll see you Saturday unless Doris decides not to come."

"Until then." Caitlin held the door open.

Mel felt Caitlin's gaze on her as she walked to her car. She activated her keyless entry and looked up as Caitlin closed the door. It seemed her reasons for turning up on Caitlin's doorstep had run out. She prayed that Doris could be persuaded to visit. "Damn."

Chapter Six

The Status Quo

"Why do we have to have another woman here?" Phyllis complained. "We're happy just the way we are."

"Maybe she's a Nazi spy," Alice immediately responded.

"Yeah, she can't be trusted," Sophie added.

"Whoa! Hold on. Let's at least give her a chance. I don't want any whining or sabotage, you hear me? You treat her with respect."

"You don't want her here any more than we do."

"That may be but I'll be on my best behavior, as will all of you be." Caitlin looked at each woman in turn. "Am I understood?"

"Yes." The word sounded like four schoolgirls responding to a teacher's request. No, not a request. Order. It was an order.

There was a knock at the door and Caitlin walked to answer it. "Behave," she mouthed at her charges. She opened the door. "Come in!" She stood aside and allowed a petite woman with a shock of white hair to enter. Mel followed behind her.

"Good morning, everyone," Mel said brightly.

"Hi, sugar," Sophie answered in her teasing tone.

"Yeah," Phyllis replied.

"Everyone, this is Doris. She's come to meet you all."

"Who is the President of the United States?" Alice asked.

"Obama," Doris replied.

"Who?" Alice shuffled toward Mel. "I think she's a spy, Major."

"A what?" Doris looked from Alice to Mel. "What's she talking about?"

"A Nazi spy. You failed at the first question. Everyone knows the President is FDR. You should have studied up on the good old US of A."

"Corporal, she's actually an American spy." Mel was thinking on her feet. "She has been undercover for quite a while and has been out of touch with current politics."

"What's going on?" Doris asked Caitlin, who pulled her aside.

"Alice has a little dementia. She thinks she's living in World War II and she's part of the Resistance," Caitlin muttered. "Just play along."

"Uh huh."

"Dementia has never been proved." Mel saw Doris mentally withdrawing from the group. "It's not a bad place."

"Who has dementia?" Alice asked.

"A little dementia? Isn't that like saying you're a little bit pregnant?" Phyllis added.

'You have dementia," Caitlin explained. "And yes, you can have a little dementia without it being a full-blown case."

"Why didn't someone tell me?"

"We did but you don't remember it."

"I'm confused," Doris said.

"You're confused? I'm confused and I live here," Isabel explained.

"Hold it!" Mel said loudly. "Let's sit down and have a cup of coffee."

"Good idea. Come in and sit down. Coffee?" Caitlin showed Doris to the dining room table. When Doris nodded to the coffee she disappeared into the kitchen.

"Let me introduce you." Mel waited for everyone to be seated. "This is Phyllis, Alice, Isabel and Sophie. The woman who owns the place is Caitlin."

"And this is it?"

"There's only four residents in this particular retirement home. Caitlin runs the place by herself."

"Is there something wrong with it?" The women around the table bristled at Doris's comment. "I mean shouldn't there be more people?"

Mel answered before anyone else could. "Caitlin has opened up her house to these women and she looks after them. It's a highly unusual situation here."

"And what does she get in return?"

"Caitlin does this out of the goodness of her heart."

"How noble."

Phyllis rose to Caitlin's defense. "Now see here. Caitlin has been very good to us. Don't you go making snide remarks about something you know nothing about."

"Phyllis—"

"Our little family here has been doing fine without the need to include anyone else."

"Phyllis—"

"So why don't you run back to your fancy home and loving family and leave us alone!"

"Oh, boy." Mel felt her hopes disappear.

Caitlin emerged with two mugs in her hands. "What did I miss?" Mel looked at her then at Phyllis. "Oh, dear."

She put the mugs on the table and pushed one to Doris and the other to Mel. Before she said another word she made two more trips to the kitchen to collect the remaining mugs. Finally she sat down in the vacant chair.

"I don't think this is right for me," Doris said.

"Darn tootin'," Alice replied.

"I think you've got the wrong idea," Mel said.

"No, she hasn't," Phyllis interrupted. "She's got the same idea as everyone else has. Just because we're lesbians there's something wrong with this place."

"You're lesbians?"

"Oh, come on. It's on the front door, for Christ's sake!"

"Phyllis! Language."

Doris took a deep breath. "What I was trying to say is that if this is as good as you say it is, why aren't there more residents?"

"I'm only one person. Four is about the limit of what I can handle. I don't get paid for this, Doris, so I have no income to pay for food, rates, power, medicine and anything else that may arise.

We have an arrangement where their social security checks go into the kitty and we pay all our bills. Whatever is left over is theirs."

"If you had more people you could hire someone."

"I suppose I could but then the government becomes involved when there are paid employees. I don't want this to become a business. My grandma started this and I'm just carrying on her wishes. It's for those women who have nowhere else to turn."

"And who are lesbian," Doris added.

"That's coincidental."

"Yet all of you are," Doris said the words with some confidence. She received a nod in answer. "I'm not. That would change the dynamic of the home."

"We're not all sex maniacs." Phyllis's hackles rose.

"Speak for yourself," Sophie said with glee.

Doris looked horrified. "She's all bluster," Phyllis said. "Do we look like we're in any condition to be bed hopping?"

Doris looked at each woman in turn. "She does." She pointed at Alice.

"Believe me, she's probably forgotten what sex is."

"Hey!" Alice complained. "This is wartime, missy. I'm too busy keeping the enemy from our doorstep."

"This conversation is getting us nowhere."

"No, it's very informative."

"And what have you learned?" Mel asked.

"I can see that you are a family. You stick up for one another, even while you're complaining about one another. Caitlin doesn't want another resident because four is all she can handle. You feel that a straight woman will make things uncomfortable for you all. And you all think enough of Dr. Stokes to allow this interview to take place."

There was silence for a moment.

"That pretty well sums it up," Isabel said.

"Anyone want to say anything?" Caitlin asked.

"And how do you feel about this arrangement?" Alice asked the question with some clarity. Caitlin did a double take.

"I don't really know. I had come here expecting not to like it. The last year has been a strain on me. Not the housework, but the emptiness of the house. I miss the sound of a human voice."

"You could join a church group or take up a hobby."

"I don't drive so leaving the house for anything but grocery shopping is hard. My daughter will help if she's able, but lately…" Doris's voice trailed off. "What I'm looking for is some companionship and conversation to fill in the long daylight hours."

"You could get that in a normal retirement home."

Doris smiled.

"What?"

"Even you don't think this place is normal."

'The difference," Sophie said, "is that we say it with a lot of love."

"Retirement places are either selling themselves as a holiday retreat or the last stop before death." Doris added.

Mel sat back and watched the conversation unfold. She smiled behind her mug as Doris spoke. It had been a long time since she had seen the woman so animated. She'd been right. Her eyes met Caitlin and they both grinned.

"This one is Churchill's last defense," Alice announced. "And no one is going to breach its walls."

"Not even an ally?" Mel asked.

Alice studied Doris with a critical eye. "Until she can prove to me she is indeed a Yankee, no, not even her."

"Drinking rum and coca cola," Doris warbled, making them all laugh.

Even Phyllis found it amusing. "Touché."

Mel's beeper went off. She fumbled around her bag and pulled out the unit. "It looks like I've got an emergency."

"Go, we'll be fine." Caitlin stood and waited for Mel to move. "I'm sure we can keep her amused."

"I'm sure you can. I'm sorry, Doris. I hope I won't be long. If I am, I'll call."

"Fine, Dr. Stokes." Doris gave her an uncertain look for a second before plastering on a sunny smile.

Mel stepped out of the house and into the sunshine. She didn't like to leave Doris alone, but she had no choice. While she had made a little progress in getting both sides interested in one another, she hoped that her efforts to place Doris in the home didn't go off the rails while she was away. Mel hopped into her car. This would have to be a fast visit. How fast could she drive without attracting the police or ending up in hospital?

Chapter Seven

Thinking Out Loud

"So," Caitlin closed the door and turned to find five pairs of eyes looking at her. "What'll we do?"

Phyllis stood and stiffly walked toward the back door. "I'm going to sit outside for a while."

"Come on," Caitlin begged, "can't we do something together? Something that'll help us to get to know one another?"

"How about spin the bottle?" Sophie asked hopefully.

"No."

"Pin the bikini on the model?"

"No."

"Scrabble®?"

"Definitely no."

"I can play that."

"Believe me, Doris, you do *not* want to play Scrabble® with these women."

"Why not?"

"I'll even keep it clean."

"Sophie, don't go making promises you have no intention of keeping."

"What's going on?"

"Let's just say you would get a very explicit lesbian education if you played Scrabble® with these women."

"Oh."

"What else is there?" Sophie asked. "We've exhausted all our options."

"Then we'll have to invent new ones." Caitlin tried to sound enthusiastic but she knew it would be a hard task to engage their interest.

"What other board games have you got?"

"Only Monopoly. I usually don't have the spare cash to buy such things."

"If I joined, you may be able to buy a new thing or two for the house."

Caitlin watched Doris with interest. "You've changed your mind?"

"Just thinking out loud. I'm not the sort of person who butts in where she's not wanted."

"I didn't mean that. As I said I'm comfortable with the four women I have, but that doesn't mean that five wouldn't work either. If we went out on a day trip somewhere you may get to know Sophie better than you ever wanted to."

"I've got a car at home that I don't use. My daughter wants to sell it and I've been tempted to do just that. It's one of those big things that carry six or eight. Norman was a typical male in that respect. The bigger the car—"

"Yeah, they never get it, do they?"

Doris laughed.

"It'll be a while before Dr. Stokes gets back. How about I show you round? You know, in case you're thinking out loud again." Caitlin extended her hand toward the hall. "Sophie, keep out of trouble."

"Me? What did I do?"

"I don't know. You tell me."

"Cross my heart, I didn't do a thing."

"Right," Caitlin said sarcastically. "I bet plenty was going on in your mind though."

"What goes on in my mind stays in my mind."

Caitlin walked away laughing. She knew Sophie's fertile thoughts had a way of inserting themselves into real life, whether Sophie had intended them to or not.

"So far I've managed to give each lady a room to themselves."

"And me?"

"I think I can squeeze out one more."

"How many rooms does this place have?"

"It's pretty big. Grandma was raised in this house and she was one of thirteen kids."

"Thirteen?"

"Yep. When they moved in here there was nothing but vacant fields. Grandpa added the rooms as they were needed and it grew into this."

"I'm surprised developers haven't tried to move in."

"They had, but Grandma was a stubborn old bird. We've kept the wolves from our door, but only just." Caitlin moved past the occupied rooms to a newer section of the house. "You can have this room if you like. If you want to be closer to the others, we'll see if someone is prepared to move." When Doris didn't answer, Caitlin continued, "I'll ask."

"What could I bring?"

"Anything you want to make it your own room is fine, so long as it doesn't block the way to your bed. We don't want the doctor climbing over furniture to get to you. What do you have in mind?"

"Just thinking out loud," Doris said, then winked at Caitlin.

"Right."

†

"How did it go?" Mel arrived two hours later to find Doris sharing a coffee with Caitlin. "Don't you do anything else but make coffee?"

"What can I say? I like the stuff."

"You better watch it around here, Doris. Before you know it she'll have you guzzling coffee down like water."

"And that's a bad thing?"

"Yes, if you want to live to be seventy." Mel sat down. "So, how did it go?"

"Doris is doing a lot of 'thinking out loud', so it's promising."

"Thinking out loud?"

"Never mind."

"Doris, any thoughts?"

"I don't know. It's such a big step."

"How about a trial for a week?" Mel waited for confirmation from both women. "Then you can re-consider your options if you need to."

"What about my house?"

"I'm sure it can survive without you for a week. Just leave out food and water and it'll be fine."

"The woman thinks she's a comedienne."

"We only want you to feel comfortable with your decision. It won't be final until you say so."

"What about a bed?"

"Hmmm, I hadn't thought of that."

"If it's only for a week, I can sleep on the couch."

"You shouldn't have to do that," Doris complained.

"It's either you or me, and I'm a lot younger than you."

"I think I saw a foldaway bed at the Community Center. Let me look into it." Mel looked expectantly at Caitlin and Doris. "What do you think?"

"I'm prepared to give it a go if you are," Caitlin said.

Doris sighed. "All right. For a week."

Mel reached into her bag and pulled out a box of hair dye. "Maybe this will help smooth the way."

"I like my hair the way it is, Dr. Stokes."

"It's not for you."

"How did you know…?"

"I saw the box in Phyllis's waste paper bin. I figured if she was in a better mood things might not be so prickly."

"She'll kiss you," Caitlin said as she accepted the dye.

"A handshake will do fine, thanks."

†

After Doris and Mel left, Caitlin called a meeting to announce the news.

"It looks like we'll have another resident."

"Why did you agree to that? Aren't we happy just the way we are?"

"I'm telling you, no good will come of this," Alice announced. "I'll send a wireless message to London to get her credentials."

"A new woman… hee hee hee." Sophie giggled. She was way too happy about the situation.

"Listen to me, all of you. You are not to harass, seduce or interrogate her." Caitlin growled. "You all know what it's like to be in a minority, and she'll be one here. Treat her with the respect you each once pleaded for." Caitlin stood up and walked into the kitchen.

"She's right, you know," Isabel said.

"It doesn't make it any easier to accept. Awww, hell!" Phyllis struggled to stand and shuffled off to her bedroom.

"What's crawled up her butt?"

"She must be missing the wheelchair."

Caitlin returned. "Where's Phyllis?"

"She stomped off."

"I'll need one of you to swap rooms for the week. Sophie, could you?"

"Why does it have to be me?"

"Because you have the least amount of junk to move."

"That's so not fair. I've finally gotten the room the way I want it."

"Sophie," Caitlin said, "you're not moving house. It's just for the week Doris is here. Besides, the girlie pictures on the wall do not constitute 'home, sweet home'. I'm sure she'd be very happy if you took them with you."

"Heaven help us if we ever get the internet," Isabel mumbled as she wandered off.

"Internet? Really?" Sophie followed her. "Where did you hear that?"

"We are *not* getting the internet," Caitlin yelled, before she spoke to herself. "I, for one, don't want to be drowning in porn." Suddenly she felt sad. "Hell, I can't even get a proper date."

Caitlin trudged down the hallway to Phyllis's room. "I've got a present for you."

"That woman's not coming? Best news I've had all week."

"Sorry, no. The doctor asked me to pass this onto you." Caitlin tossed the box onto Phyllis's bed.

Phyllis looked at the box then Caitlin. "Trying to butter me up?"

"Can't get anything by you," Caitlin muttered before she left the room.

She walked back up the hallway to the dining room. It was way too quiet and Caitlin was alone. She had a glimpse of what Doris felt and didn't like it. Having been surrounded by people yakking at her all the time she hoped that at the end of her life it didn't come to this. Suddenly it seemed important to make Doris welcome.

†

Monday came and went and no sign of Doris. Had she changed her mind? Mel hadn't called saying so, so maybe there was a hiccup in the transport.

Tuesday morning rolled around and still no Doris. Caitlin started to worry. She found her cell and dialed the number Mel gave her.

"Stokes," Mel answered abruptly.

"Hi, it's me." There was a hesitation and Caitlin responded. "Caitlin."

"Hi." Mel sounded distracted.

"I was expecting Doris yesterday. Has something happened?"

"She didn't arrive? Shit!"

Caitlin heard a muffled sound and 'sorry.', obviously spoken to someone who was with Mel.

"I'm sorry. I've disturbed you. Call me—"

"No! No, it's all right. Let me call her and I'll get back to you. Bye."

Before Caitlin had a chance to respond Mel hung up. "Bye," she said to the dead connection. "Okaaay." She put her cell down on the sideboard and walked away, before turning her thoughts to the day's chores.

†

Mel was in a tizz. She had thought that Doris was ready to go, but obviously she was wrong. Sandra had not been happy about the arrangement until she had at least seen the place, but Doris seemed determined to have her own way.

She looked across at Alex. "Can we talk later? It seems I have a slight emergency."

"What about Mrs. Campbell?"

"Check with Caroline and book an appointment. If there isn't a free one today, I'll see her at the end of the day."

"Great, thanks Mel." Alex stood and collected the patient's file sitting on Mel's desk. "You can call your girlfriend back."

"My what? I think you've got the wrong idea," Mel tried to sound indignant.

Alex smiled. "I don't think so." He started to leave before she could deny it any further. She chuckled as he looked over his shoulder and wiggled his eyebrows. "You are a troublemaker," she said.

"So I've been told," he replied as he closed the door.

Mel's smile dropped. She rubbed her hands over her face. What the hell had gone wrong? She suspected that Sandra had something to do with it, but until she called Doris it was only speculation.

Mel went to her filing cabinet and found Doris's file. She opened it and her finger slid down the page until she found the number she was looking for. It was not a call she wanted to make, but she knew she had to. "Shit," she whispered. Grabbing the cell, Mel punched in the numbers. It rang three times. She was about to hang up on the fourth when the call was answered.

"Hello?"

"Doris?"

"Yes, who is this?"

"It's Dr. Stokes. I got a call from Caitlin to say you didn't arrive yesterday."

"Yes, well, you see it's Sandra—"

"Doris, we've been through this before. It's your decision, not hers."

"I know, dear, but she thinks it might be better—"

"And what do you think, Doris?" Mel interrupted. She was losing the battle. "Has she seen the place yet?"

"She said she had and now she doesn't approve. It's so run down."

Mel's hand rose to her temple and she rubbed her skin. A headache was beginning to form. "Sandra looked at it from the outside, Doris. She didn't go inside. I think it'll be a good placement for you."

"But Sandra—"

"I'll talk to Sandra. In the meantime, pack enough things for a week." Mel pressed her case and hoped Doris wouldn't argue. She knew she would get plenty of that from her daughter.

"If you say so."

Mel could hear the confusion in Doris's voice. "Everything will be fine. If, at the end of the week, you don't like the place then I won't mention it again. Okay?"

"Fine, dear."

"Thanks, Doris. I'll call Sandra now and we'll sort this out. I'll be in touch." Mel hung up the phone and leaned back in her chair. Mel felt guilty pushing Doris into the home. The woman had crawled back into her shell and was willing to be subservient to whoever tried to make decisions for her. Had she any more right than Sandra to push the issue? She wanted to make sure Doris would be happy, but wasn't Sandra doing the same?

Before she made the call Mel went looking for a fresh cup of coffee.

"You don't look happy," Caroline said from her seat behind the reception desk.

Mel gazed at the woman who ran her office. Caroline was a solidly built woman in her mid-forties who had the face of an angel. Mel didn't know what she'd do without her.

Mel placed her mug on the desk and buried her head in her hands.

"What's wrong?"

"Mrs. Hansen."

"She's the one going to the lesbian retirement home."

"It's that you remember?"

"It's the one I'm going with." Caroline stood up and grabbed Mel's mug. She walked to the coffee machine and filled it for her, putting in the cream and sugar before stirring. For good measure, she grabbed a cookie from the cookie jar. "There you go," she said as she delivered the goods.

"Thanks. She didn't make it to the home."

"What? She had a heart attack?"

"More a daughter attack."

"Ahh, now I see. It's phone the relative time."

Mel nodded. "It's not going to be pretty."

The phone rang. "It never is," Caroline said before she answered it.

Mel grabbed her coffee and cookie and returned to her office. The file was still open and she gazed at Sandra's phone number. God, she hated these calls. She took a bite out of her cookie as she continued to stare at the number. What would she say? Maybe Sandra would start the conversation and she would jump in at the appropriate time. When the cookie ran out she knew that her delay tactic had also.

She put down her coffee and lifted the receiver. "Damn," she muttered. The phone rang twice.

"Carroll and Wilson."

"Sandra Boyer, please."

"One moment."

The phone muzak annoyed the hell out of her as she waited. A full minute had gone by and she was about to hang up when a familiar voice answered.

"Sandra Boyer."

"Sandra? It's Dr. Stokes."

"Hello."

That was all she said. 'Hello.' It spoke volumes. "I was wondering why Doris isn't at the home today."

"I thought that was obvious. She changed her mind."

Mel was so tempted to say, no, *you* changed her mind, but she didn't want to get into a shouting match.

"We've discussed this before."

"Look, Doctor, she doesn't want to go. Why can't you accept that?"

"Because I was with her when she visited that place. She seemed quite happy about at least trying it for a week. Why can't you let her decide for herself?"

"Just like you do?"

"It's not good for her mental health to be in that big house all alone. At Shady Oakes she has the company of four lovely ladies."

"Four lesbians, you mean."

"They're still people, Sandra."

"And they're by themselves in that place. Doesn't that tell you something?"

"Like what?" Mel demanded. Her blood pressure slowly rose.

"They're not fit to be around normal people."

God, she hated these people. Mel kept her anger in check. "I don't appreciate your comments."

"That's not my problem. I don't want her going there."

"If she agrees, she can still keep her house."

"That's unlikely. Retirement places are expensive. The only way she can afford it is if she sells the house."

"Shady Oakes only charges a nominal fee. Your mother could lease out her house and use the rent to pay for the home expenses."

"There's no point in keeping the house." Sandra said flatly. "Or the car."

But it can fill up your bank account, Mel thought. She had long suspected that Sandra was after her parents' money.

"The home is nearby to where you live. You'd be able to visit her often." Mel was running out of ideas.

"That's not an issue. I want her in a nice nursing home."

"You mean 'retirement' home," Mel corrected.

"They're both the same."

"No they're not." Mel contemplated the coffee sitting on her desk. "We can argue about this all day, but I can see your mind is made up. I've convinced Doris to go for the week. If, after that time, she doesn't want to go back I won't mention it again."

"Good."

The line went dead.

"Of all the…" Mel slammed the phone down and deliberately banged her head on the table a number of times. A steady heartbeat thumped in her brain. "Bitch!" she yelled.

There was a knock at the door and Caroline peeked around the corner. "Everything okay?" she asked tentatively.

"No, everything is *not* okay," Mel ground out.

Chapter Eight

A Week in the Life...

Caitlin answered the knock on the door. "Hello! Glad to see that you finally made it." She stepped aside and allowed Doris and Mel to step inside. "You can have Sophie's room for the week."

"She'll be staying until Sunday. Her daughter will pick her up."

Caitlin heard the anger in Mel's voice and gave her a questioning look. "Sunday? That's only five days."

"Sorry, that was the best I could do."

"Isabel!" Caitlin called. The small woman walked toward her. "Could you show Doris to her room?"

"Sure," Isabel said meekly, "This way." She turned and shuffled away, expecting that Doris would follow her.

"Thanks, Dr. Stokes. Will I see you soon?"

"I'll keep in touch."

Mel and Caitlin watched the two women walk up the hallway and disappear into Sophie's room.

"Sophie!" Isabel screamed.

"What?" Sophie yelled back.

Caitlin sighed.

"Do you want to move your pin-up babes off the wall?"

"Jeez—" Sophie stopped in mid curse when she spotted Caitlin. "Why certainly, Isabel. I will be there in a moment." She grinned at them and entered her room.

"Oh, for crying out loud." Caitlin muttered. "Coffee?"

Mel glanced at her and shook her head. "No, I can't. I've got to get back to the office. Sorry about the bed. I thought we had a spare one."

"The sofa won't kill me."

"It might. Those things are nasty when they're in a bad mood."

As Mel made a move toward the door, Caitlin blurted out, "When will I see you again?"

"I don't know. I have a pretty full schedule this week. Doris's daughter will pick her up on Sunday, so unless there's an emergency it might be a while."

"I was thinking of taking them out for a picnic on Saturday. Do you want to come along?"

"Well, I…hang on. You can't fit them all into your car."

Caitlin looked at her shyly. "I was kind of hoping that you could help me with that."

"So, I'm nothing more than a chauffeur, huh?" Despite the words, Mel smiled.

"I'll throw in lunch for free. Does that help?"

"I don't know. What sort of lunch?" Mel's eyes twinkled.

"The sort you eat." Mel pursed her lips. "What? You want a liquid lunch?"

"What time?"

"Is noon okay?"

"Fine. I'll see you then."

After Mel left Caitlin leaned against the door. "Now what did I say?"

✝

Phyllis sat outside to take in the rays of the morning sun that slanted across the back porch. The heat soon increased and she was forced to remove her cardigan. The tattoos on her forearms, faded with age, glared back at her and reminded her of a time when all she lived for was the sun on her back and the wind in her hair.

She reminisced about her old bike. It had carried her many miles, from Washington to Dallas, Los Angeles to Portland and everywhere in between. It was the only family she knew for many years.

"Sophie!"

She heard Isabel's yell, and Sophie's response, and wondered what new catastrophe had happened. A couple of minutes later the back screen door swung outward and Doris stepped out. She sat down on the bench against the wall.

Phyllis looked at her. "Problem?"

"Sophie has pinups of girls on the wall."

"It's a hobby of hers."

"She kept giggling to herself. Should I be worried?"

"Of Sophie? Nah! She's just kidding... mostly."

"She's not going to do something, is she?"

"Something?"

"You know, like trying to kiss me."

"I don't know. She can't break a hip kissing, but she could sprain her lips." Phyllis smiled at Doris's look of horror. "Relax. She's pulling your leg."

"Like you with your pink hair." Doris leaned back and looked at the vegetable garden.

"It was an accident."

"Uh huh."

"Do I look like the sort of person who would dye her hair pink on purpose?"

"I don't know you at all, so you might be."

"Take my word for it. I'm not."

"And yet here you are."

Phyllis couldn't argue with that. "They bought the wrong hair dye."

"And you didn't look at the packet before you used it," Doris responded.

Phyllis smiled. "You're a smart ass. I like a smart ass. Besides, I've got some new hair dye and shortly this color will be a thing of the past."

"What happened to your finger?"

"What? This?" Phyllis deliberately raised the splinted finger at Doris and wondered if the woman understood the message. "I had an accident a while back, which resulted in this."

"Is this place dangerous? It sure is strange."

"You mean us." Phyllis's smile dropped. She had hoped all the harassment had stopped, but apparently not.

"Well, yes… no. I've never seen a retirement home like this before."

"Or the fact that we're all lesbians."

"Does that include Caitlin?"

Phyllis thought for a moment. "Now that you mention it, we just assumed that she was." Her hand came up to her chin.

"That may change things," she muttered.

"Change what?" Phyllis edged a little closer.

"I, err…" Doris noticed Phyllis's subtle move and shifted slightly in her chair. "I'm not… errr…"

"The word is 'lesbian', Doris. It's not a dirty word and you won't go to Hell for saying it out loud."

Doris was mildly amused. "You point is well taken."

"Now you're looking for a place to live."

Doris looked at her hands sitting in her lap. "I lost my husband about a year ago."

"Sorry," Phyllis said.

"So was I. Forty-four years we were together. We had one child and have two lovely grandchildren." Doris sighed loudly. "Sandra's got her own place now and I was in that house all alone."

"You should have sold up and moved to somewhere like Florida. Live it up before you forget what 'living it up' means."

"My daughter thinks that sort of behavior is abhorrent."

"Abhorrent?" *That bitch*, Phyllis thought.

"Distasteful."

"I know what abhorrent means. I'm sort of surprised by her reaction though. It's your house and your life. You should be able to live it as you like."

"Like you?" Doris pointed out.

Phyllis's gaze roamed across the tattoos again. "I suppose so, but I'd probably do a thing or two different."

"Let me guess. You were a… what is it they call it? A motorcycle babe?"

Phyllis chuckled. "Dyke on a bike."

"Catchy."

"We thought so at the time."

"You were what my mother would have called a 'bad girl'."

"Damn straight, although I didn't steal or kill. I just liked the life on the road."

"Did you have a biker chick on the back?"

Phyllis laughed out loud. "Where do you hear this stuff?"

"I went to a very informative college back then."

"I dropped out at fourteen. They couldn't teach me anything more. Besides, I sort of came out around then and it was unhealthy for me to stick around."

"What about your family?"

Phyllis picked at some non-existent lint on her cardigan. "We agreed that it was best that I leave. That was the last time I ever saw them."

"Oh, Lord! How did you live?"

"You learn to survive very quickly or you die." Phyllis didn't elaborate any further.

"And you finally ended up here. How?"

"Caitlin's grandma, Ellen, owned this place and she opened it up to homeless old women. She didn't charge anything for looking after us, so we made an arrangement with her to keep the place going. However, since Caitlin took over she looks after any money left over so we don't fritter it away."

"Fritter?"

"I don't smoke anymore."

"Ahh. So that explains all the talk about social security."

"It's not much, but both Ellen and Caitlin have made this our home. It's a full time job for them so they can't earn any wages. We just get by."

"And the lesbian 'thing', I suppose it deters any more residents?"

"The lesbian 'thing', as you call it," Phyllis inwardly smiled when Doris cringed, "probably has something to do with it. The sign outside was changed by the local kids. Caitlin gave up trying to fix it."

"Still, if she sold the place, she'd make a mint. The size of the land could house an apartment block."

"Then where would we go?" Phyllis said out loud before she realized how selfish that sounded.

"She could move further out and buy a place for far less than what she would get for this place."

"No, her heart is in this house. She was practically raised here."

"So, it's a matter of the heart."

"Yeah, a matter of the heart."

Chapter Nine

Picnics and Grenades

Mel arrived precisely at noon on Saturday. She knocked on the door and waited for an answer. The sky was clear and it looked perfect for a picnic. She was surprised to see Doris answer the door. "Hi, Doris. How are you?"

"Fine, Dr. Stokes. Please, come in." She stepped aside to let Mel enter.

"Nearly ready!" Caitlin yelled from the kitchen. "Sophie! Isabel! Get your butts moving!"

"Hold on to your bra, we're coming!" Phyllis yelled back.

Caitlin carried a large basket to the front door. "Hey, glad to see you could make it."

"I said I'd be here."

"Can you take Phyllis and her wheelchair?"

"They've replaced it already?"

Caitlin wrestled the damaged wheelchair to the door. "The brake is broken and one wheel is bent on her old one, but as long as she doesn't try to do wheelies I think it's safe to sit in."

"Have you been contacted by the insurance company yet?"

"They say at least three weeks to process the claim."

"Three weeks? What the hell are they doing? Swimming to China to get the parts?" For some reason, Mel was irritated by the news. No, she knew the reason. She felt her generosity had been abused. Caitlin didn't say, 'I'd like you to come to the picnic'. No, it was, 'I need another car to transport them'. She wanted it to be a personal invitation, not a taxi service. She plastered on a smile.

"Doris, what did you do this week?"

"Doris introduced us to the local library. As soon as we get our library cards, we can go visit as often as we like," Caitlin said.

"Good news." Mel glanced at Doris and saw a smile on her lips.

"We couldn't get one for Doris yet because she's new to the area, but she can borrow on our cards in the meantime."

"Yet?" Mel looked from Doris to Caitlin.

"That's if Doris decides to stay."

Mel waited expectantly for Doris to say something, but she remained quiet. "Let's wait and see," Mel answered for her.

She pushed Phyllis's wheelchair to her car and wrestled it into the trunk. By the time she returned most the women were assembled.

"What took you so long?" Phyllis complained.

"I... ahh, what's the point," Mel said grumpily.

"What's got up her ass?" Sophie whispered.

"Search me," Phyllis replied.

"Could you take this, please?" Caitlin handed the basket to Mel.

"Sure," Mel said, but it was a less than enthusiastic response.

Finally Alice turned up dressed in dark pants and shirt. *A good combination for subterfuge*, Mel thought. "Let's get this show on the road. Follow me." Mel walked out the front door, fully expecting Phyllis to follow her. The older woman moved slowly to the car, pain etched on her features with every step. Mel stood at the car waiting for Phyllis to arrive. Suddenly she felt very petty. Phyllis was struggling and she was whining about an absent 'thank you'. She extended her hand and steadied Phyllis as she took her seat in the car.

Mel closed the door and trotted around to the driver's side. "Grow up, Mel" she muttered. If she had been honest with herself, it was a good excuse to see Caitlin again, but as far as she could see her subtle romantic hints were getting her nowhere.

"Buckle up," she said as she did just that.

Phyllis glared at her. "I've been waiting here for you to finally show up. Lose you way to the driver's seat?"

"Yeah. Had to leap frog over that heap you call a wheelchair."

Surprisingly, Phyllis laughed out loud. "You know, sometimes you're almost tolerable."

"Gee, thanks for the compliment."

At that moment Caitlin's station wagon roared into life and slowly backed out of the driveway.

"Do you know where we're going?" Mel asked.

"I thought you knew that," Phyllis replied before plastering on a wicked smile. "If we lose 'em we can always find a bar."

"You and me out on a date, huh?"

"No, but I may get lucky with some young chick."

Mel glanced at her. "And what are you going to do with her? Maybe you'll need an extendable arm for those hard to reach places."

"Doc! How rude!" But that didn't stop a quiet chuckle escaping Phyllis's lips. "Maybe I should suggest that to Sophie for your date."

Mel blanched. "I'm going to live to regret this, aren't I?"

"Yup."

"Oh God, kill me now!"

"At least wait until I'm out of the car."

As much as she didn't want to admit it, Mel liked Phyllis. The woman may have been grumpy, but she certainly showed a lot of spunk. Would she have ended up like her if she'd followed her heart and took to the road on a bike?

"Hey!" Phyllis barked. "You better get your mind back on the road." She pointed out the front window as Caitlin's car turned the far corner.

Mel shifted the gear into drive and took off after the disappearing Chevy. The car slew around the corner and straightened up with a wiggle. "Christ! Where does she think she is? Indy?"

"You're losing her."

"I know! I know!" Mel drove as fast as she dared but couldn't seem to catch up to Caitlin. She swerved around another corner. "Damn." The car slowed as they looked down one side street and another for a flash of yellow. Mel was about to give up when she spotted the Chevy. Praying that there wasn't a cop around, Mel turned the steering wheel wildly to make the right-hand turn. The car pulled up with a screech.

Mel sat back and took a deep breath. "God!" she groaned.

"Nice parking." Phyllis looked out the window and saw she was a good foot and a half from the curb.

Mel held up her hand. "Give me a moment." She closed her eyes and waited for her heart rate to drop to triple figures.

Phyllis laughed. "You are such a wuss."

There was a knock on the passenger side window. Phyllis opened it and Caitlin smiled brightly at them. "What took you so long?"

"Stopped for a beer," Mel said straight-faced. She tried not to cry.

"Really?" Caitlin opened the door. "Can you grab Phyllis's wheelchair?"

Shakily, Mel got out and stumbled to the back of the car. Her heart still beat at a blistering pace and it took a moment or two before she popped open the trunk.

"Where did you learn to drive?" she asked.

"Grandma was a good teacher."

"And you got your license on the first try?"

"What do you mean by that? I'm a very good driver."

A pithy remark sat on Mel's tongue and it took all her strength not to say it. Instead she lifted the wheelchair out of the back.

"She thinks you drive fast," Phyllis offered.

Mel glared at Phyllis, who grinned back at her. "Thanks for nothing," she muttered.

"Are you saying that I have a lead foot?"

"No... no, I'd never say that."

"But she'd think it."

"Phyllis!" Mel hands gripped the wheelchair, wondering if she could get away with aggravated assault. "Stop helping!"

"Just telling it like it is, Doc."

"Then f-f-f-f-... for crying out loud, stop telling."

Caitlin grabbed the wheelchair from Mel's grasp and lifted it up onto the sidewalk. She opened it up and held it steady as Phyllis took her seat. "Hrrmp," Caitlin sniffed at her and pushed Phyllis to the picnic table, giving Mel an evil stare over her shoulder.

"Great. Just great." Mel pushed the button on her keyless entry and followed a few steps behind.

Doris met Mel half-way to the seats and whispered, "Can I go back with you?"

"Why?" But she knew why. Caitlin was a maniac on the road.

"Because that small woman... you know, the one who thinks she's an assassin or something."

"Alice—"

"Yes, Alice. She kept talking about secret missions, crossing the border and taking hostages." Doris looked nervously about. "And the other one..."

"Isabel? Sophie?"

"The nymphomaniac."

"Sophie."

"...Sophie kept giggling. I was nearly in that poor woman's lap, I was so scared."

"Sophie's lap?" Mel was surprised.

"No, the other one."

"Alice?"

"No. The... other... one." Doris replied, saying each word succinctly.

"Isabel."

"I think I may have squashed her."

"I doubt it. That would have been the first thing Caitlin would have mentioned." Mel patted Doris's arm. "Look, they're just having some fun with you."

"I don't think so. The assassin glared at me the whole time. She's not convinced I'm an ally."

Mel knew her chances of placing Doris were slipping away. "Come with me." She walked with Doris past the table and continued on to the next one fifty feet away. "Take a seat." Caitlin looked at her with concern and she waved back at her. Mel marshaled her thoughts while Doris sat down.

"I don't think I'm going to fit in here, Dr. Stokes."

"I understand your concern, Doris. It took me a little while to get used to them. Let me reassure you that they mean you no harm." The words sounded worse than she had intended, coming out as a passive threat.

"Maybe Sandra was right."

Mel so wanted Sandra to be wrong, and that thought horrified her. Was she more intent on winning than finding a safe haven for her patient?

"Why is it so important that I go to this place?"

"I don't know. I just have a good feeling about Shady Oakes. I'm worried that if you go into a different retirement home you'll wither away and die." Mel saw Doris wince. "Sorry, I don't mean to sound morbid, but you need people your own age around you who will remind you that you still have plenty of wonderful and active years left in you. These are people who will stimulate your mind, and they'll certainly keep you laughing with their antics."

"They scare me." Mel was at a loss for words, so she sat silently and waited for Doris to continue. "Caitlin is nice, but the others…"

"Do you remember what it was like when you were a kid and someone new came to the school?" Doris nodded. "Well, you're that new kid. They have to get used to you just as you have to get used to them. They've been together as a group for a while now and an outsider has them skittish."

"Then maybe I should look elsewhere."

"Do you really want to do that?" It was a dangerous question to ask, but Mel felt she needed to lay her cards on the table. "Think about this. If you want to stay here you won't have to sell your house. You can rent it out. If things get too much you can always move back home." Mel leaned forward and rested her arms on the table. "But if you decide to go with a regular retirement home you'll probably have to sell your place. They require bonds, contracts and such and the fees will be a lot higher. There will be no going back from there."

"I… I don't know."

"You don't have to decide now, but don't wait too long." Once Sandra picked Doris up Mel knew she could no longer offer any advice or support. Doris would be at the mercy of her daughter. "Come on, let's get something to eat." Mel rose and helped Doris to her feet. They strolled back to the group to join the picnic.

†

"You made your mind up yet?" Phyllis asked casually as she and Doris sat at the picnic table alone. Her gaze swept to the far side of the park where two small groups of women were walking along the path surrounding it. Caitlin was in the lead with an eager Alice, while Mel followed a hundred or so feet behind with Isabel and Sophie. She cast a glance at Doris. "Hmmm?"

"I don't think this is right for me."

"I thought you were having fun this week."

"I was, but—"

"Don't let them scare you. They're pussycats." Phyllis looked down at her hands. "Or is it me you're scared of?" She looked at Doris frankly.

"You? Why would I be scared of you?"

"Because I'm the unofficial leader of this gang." Phyllis hesitated. "Do I scare you?"

"A little bit."

"Don't be. I know I'm a bit gruff sometimes, but underneath I'm a softie."

"You could have fooled me. Why do you care what happens to me?"

Phyllis looked away and watched the women continuing their walk. She shrugged. "I suppose I don't. I was just asking."

"Really?"

"Look," Phyllis turned her attention to Doris, "I'm sorry if we've been a bit strange."

"A bit?"

"All right. A lot strange. We've gotten used to how we are and have forgotten how it can look to outsiders."

"And I'm an outsider?"

65

"You don't have to be."

Phyllis watched Doris's eyes widen. "Is that an invitation?"

Phyllis's fingers fiddled with a loose thread on her shirt. "Maybe." Her fingers pulled harshly and the thread came loose. "I don't want you to blame the doc for this. She really is trying to help you."

"And how long have you known Dr. Stokes?"

"Errr…" Phyllis tried to do the mental arithmetic. "About three weeks?"

Doris laughed. "I've known her for five years, so I think I know her better than you do." Phyllis opened her mouth but Doris held up her hand. "Don't worry, I agree with you. She has been nothing but helpful to me in that time."

"What's she like?"

"Professional and efficient. I didn't get much of a chance to see her outside the consulting room."

"I suppose we have the advantage of her coming to us for that."

"Alice is a bit scary. Has she hurt anyone?"

"Not seriously. She terrorized the dog next door once and I think there was a gerbil a few years ago. Otherwise, she's living in her own little world."

"And yet she interacts with you all. Strange sort of dementia."

"If it's dementia at all."

"Hasn't the doctor checked her out?"

"We can't afford the tests. Besides, she's happy the way she is and we don't mind."

"And if she snaps?"

"Then we'll pick up the pieces and put her back together again. We won't abandon her just because things get tough."

There was silence for a while and Phyllis looked at Doris. "Are you okay?"

"Sure, just thinking."

†

"Alice, slow down!"

"Damned Nazis!" Alice growled. She trotted off into the trees sitting next to the path.

"Where are you going?" Caitlin broke into a slow jog as she tried to keep sight of her charge.

"I'm looking for booby traps and land mines. Be careful." Alice's voice carried on the wind back to her.

"She's trying to kill me. I know it," she muttered.

"Over here, Captain," Alice yelled. She picked up an empty soda can. "Hand grenade." She put the can to her lips, as if she was ripping out the pin, then threw it. "Get down!" Alice hit the dirt and covered her head.

"Alice. Come on. Stop playing in the dirt." Caitlin walked to her and helped her to stand.

"But, Captain."

"It's time to go home." She gently guided Alice back to the path and encouraged her to continue on. She wanted to be home before Christmas.

✝

"So, Doc." Sophie sidled up beside Mel. "When is our date? Where are you taking me?"

Mel heard Isabel's chuckle and glared at her. "Don't encourage her."

"I didn't say a thing."

"You didn't have to. I heard that snicker."

"You've been teasing me long enough and I want some action."

"Oh, Lord." Mel stopped walking. "Look, Sophie, I think this has gone on long enough. You and I both know I was playing along. I'm sorry."

Sophie looked at her, her face a mixture of disbelief and sadness. "Oh, Doc. You are a wicked, wicked woman." A moment later she grinned. "I'm just razzing you."

"Oh, that's a relief," Mel breathed deeply and let out her tension.

"We both know this was meant to be. Don't try getting out of our date."

"What?!" Mel wished there was a wall nearby so she could pound her head against it.

Isabel stepped up next to her and whispered, "She's joking."

"You are such an easy target." Sophie patted Mel's back as she doubled over.

"You're killing me here."

"Hey! I'm seventy-seven years old. What else am I going to do with my time?"

"Get a hobby? So all this stuff about women…"

"No, that's very real. I'm a little more subtle about it."

"Subtle?" Mel didn't think Sophie had ever been subtle about anything, least of all about her sexuality.

"Sure. The idea is to catch a woman, not drive her away." Sophie said. "Although not being able to get out of the house often does have a way of stifling my opportunities."

Mel shook her head. The home was truly a nuthouse and she momentarily wondered if placing Doris in the middle of it was a good idea. "How do you put up with this?" she said to Isabel.

"I tend to switch off."

"What do you do to keep yourself busy?"

"Lots and lots of crosswords."

"And a mean Scrabble® player I bet."

"I don't get the chance to play it properly."

"Let me ask you this, if you had a windfall what would you spend it on?"

"We've won the lottery? That's pretty good, and we didn't even buy a ticket." Sophie clapped her hands with glee.

"It was just a question."

"What sort of amount are we talking about?" Isabel asked, her eyes narrowing with interest.

"I don't know. A thousand dollars? Ten thousand dollars? What would you add to the place?"

"This isn't teasing, it's torture. You're waving the veritable carrot in front of our faces."

Mel blinked. That was the most she had heard Isabel say in one go. "Don't you ever dream?"

"I do, but I've found it's not good to dream too wildly. At this point, I'm glad to get up the next morning."

"You didn't answer the question. I'm talking about something or things that would benefit you all, and not be for just yourself."

"A computer," Isabel answered.

"Interesting answer. Why a computer? I would have thought that you girls were a bit past a computer."

"Oh, yeah. Porn. I'll take Isabel's answer."

Mel sighed. You could take the girl out of the porn but you couldn't take the porn out of the girl. "You have a one-track mind."

"Hey." Sophie shrugged. "It's who I am."

"And you're scaring the life out of Doris. Be nice."

"Before I moved to Shady Oakes I was what you would call a 'computer nerd'. I wasn't very good with people, so I kept to myself and my computer."

Mel nodded as Isabel spoke. She didn't want to stop her speaking because she knew the woman was using a year's worth of conversation.

"What did you do? Work for a big computer company?"

"I was a professor of mathematics."

"A professor? Wow." She was impressed. "Hang on, if you were a professor then you would have taught face-to-face classes."

"I wasn't that sort of professor. I dealt with the theoretical aspects of it. I only needed my mind… and a computer."

"And you ended up at the home." Mel left the question unasked.

"I'm a spinster, Dr. Stokes. I had no interest in sex. Still don't. But I like the company."

"How did you cope with these women?"

"Hey!"

"No malice intended, Sophie."

"Malice accepted, Doc."

Isabel smiled. "It was a learning curve for all concerned. I learned to put up with the human contact and they learned to leave me alone. I think I've gotten better in the last few years, don't you think?" Isabel looked at Sophie.

"Well, that's true. When she first arrived she wouldn't play Scrabble®. Now she knows all sorts of lesbian words."

That brought up another question. Mel looked expectantly at Isabel.

"What?"

"Do I have to ask?"

"Ask what?"

"She can be a little thick at times," Sophie clucked. "She wants to know if you're a lesbian."

"As I said before I have no interest in sex, so I suppose I could be. Does that change things?" Isabel asked Sophie.

"We're looking at accepting someone who bats in the Majors. Someone sitting in the dugout doesn't bother us."

"Great baseball metaphor," Mel replied. She looked around and found that Caitlin and Alice were nearly back at the picnic table. "Come on, we're late." She steered the two women back the way they came, ushering them along like a mother hen.

Chapter Ten

When All Else Fails

"Coffee anyone?"

Mel sat in a chair back at the home trying to relax. The return trip did nothing to improve her nerves. It was only when she recognized where she was that she was content to let Caitlin out of her sight. "Please," she said.

"Doris?"

"Thank you, Caitlin. I would love one."

"I would love one?" Phyllis shook her head. "If you're going to live here, my girl, you have to loosen up."

"I'm just being polite."

"There's 'polite' and 'annoyingly polite'. Please don't stoop down to the level of the second option."

Doris faced Caitlin and said "Pleeeeaassseee." She turned to Phyllis and added, "Okay?"

Phyllis gave her the thumbs up.

Mel studied the interaction and wondered what had changed. Something definitely had. She reached for her bag. "While I've got you all here…" She pulled out six envelopes and handed one to each of the women. "…this is just to say 'thank you' for indulging me and allowing Doris to visit for this week." She sat back and waited.

"What's this?"

"An envelope. I thought you didn't have enough, so there you go."

"Okay," Caitlin raised an eyebrow at her.

"There's something inside."

71

"Really? I wonder how that happened?" Mel seriously wondered if these women had lost a few IQ points along the way. When no one moved to investigate, she prodded them. "Open it."

"It's a scratch lottery ticket."

"Give the girl a cookie." It was like leading kindergarten kids to the playground.

"What are we supposed to do with it?"

Mel was exasperated. "God! You people are... you can eat it if you want, but I found it more fun to scratch it and see if I won something."

"I don't have a coin."

Mel dug out her wallet and searched for coins. "I want these back."

"The scratchies?"

"No, the goddamned coins!"

"Language," Caitlin whispered.

"Calm blue ocean," Mel muttered. If she had been thinking straight she'd have known they were teasing her. No one was that stupid.

There was only the sound of coin scratching cardboard for a few moments.

"Hey, I won ten bucks!" Sophie said excitedly.

"Aww, damn! Nothing." Phyllis muttered.

"How about you, Alice?"

The small, wiry woman did as she was told and sat there looking at the piece of cardboard.

"No luck, huh?"

"I suppose not."

"Here, let's have a look." Phyllis snatched the scratch card out of Alice's hands and looked at it. "You haven't scratched it all off. Here, let me..." Her words died in her mouth.

"What?" Sophie asked, obviously excited by Phyllis's expression. "How much did we win?"

"Wo... wo...one thousand dollars!"

"Here," Mel grabbed the card, "let me look." Mel scratched the card a bit more. "Hmmm... sorry, Phyllis, you're wrong."

"What did you do that for? It got me all excited." Sophie whined.

"It wouldn't take—"

"Don't even go there," Phyllis said to Alice.

"How much did we win?" Alice responded.

Mel's surprised gaze rose to Alice, then to Caitlin. "Did she say what I thought she just said?"

Caitlin nodded. "She does that sometimes."

"Hey, I'm here in the room!" Alice barked.

"Doc, if you don't spill the beans right now I may just have to beat you to death with my chair."

"Sheesh, everyone is a critic."

"Now, Doc!" Phyllis yelled.

"You won five thousand dollars," Mel announced.

"No, it says one thousand." Phyllis snatched the card out of Mel's hands and pointed to the scratched windows. "See?"

"But this one has a smaller window at the bottom that you scratch and it tells you what that figure is multiplied by."

"Huh? I don't get it."

"Sophie, you never get it."

"Are you calling me stupid?"

"If the shoe fits—"

"Stop it, all of you!" Caitlin bellowed. "Now, explain it to me again."

Mel stood up and moved to Caitlin, crouching down to show her the card. "See here?" She pointed to the small scratched square at the bottom. "It says multiply the winning prize by five."

"So we really did win five thousand dollars?"

"You sure did."

"Oh, thank you." Caitlin drew Mel into a heartfelt hug, which seemed to go on forever. The hug only stopped when there was a murmuring around the table.

"Get a room, will ya."

"Sorry. I didn't mean to embarrass you." Caitlin withdrew her hands as if Mel was on fire.

"It's fine." Mel tried to dismiss it, but she really wanted the hug to continue… and continue… and continue. Caitlin was tying her up in knots and there wasn't a damned thing she could do about it. Sadly, she realized it was a hug of appreciation and nothing more. "So," Mel's voice broke on the word, "this will probably be the last time you'll see me around here."

"What?" Caitlin's mouth sagged open. "I thought you were at the community center."

"I was only relieving a colleague while he was on vacation. He returns to his duties in two weeks."

"You won't be here when Doris's daughter picks her up?" Phyllis asked.

"I think it's probably best for me not to be here. I don't want to cause a scene." Mel stood and pushed the chair closer to the table. She reached for her bag and her keys. "It has been a pleasure."

"Yeah, sure," Phyllis said.

"Err, okay. Good to meet you." Caitlin extended her hand and Mel took it. "Thanks for all your help."

It was so soft, Mel thought. She couldn't stifle the urge to caress it and her thumb idly slid over the soft V between Caitlin's thumb and finger. Mel pulled herself out of the daydream. "Anyway, take care of yourselves."

Caitlin escorted her out and waited at the door for her to walk to her car. Mel saw the door close before she muttered, "Shit." This episode on her life was now closed. Caitlin had passed her by.

†

"This sucks. It's about time Caitlin got a love life," Phyllis declared.

"Hasn't she already got one?" Isabel asked.

"Maybe she's not interested," Sophie added.

"Hellooo! Of course she's interested, but when has she had the time? She's been too busy looking after us."

"Maybe an online dating site," Isabel suggested.

"We haven't got a computer, in case you haven't noticed."

"Now that we've got some money, maybe we can."

"But Caitlin will find out."

"Do you want me to capture one of the enemy and make her go out with the captain?"

Phyllis glared at Alice. "No! No, we don't need to do that." She needed to nip that particular suggestion in the bud before Alice was arrested for a capital crime. She might be small, but she was strong and sprightly for her age, especially so when armed with her cane.

"What about the doc?" Isabel asked.

"No! Not her. She's in love with me." Sophie pleaded. "At least let me have a chance to woo her with my charm."

"She is not in love with you, you doofus. In fact, she told you to lay off." Isabel said from her point duty at the doorway.

"Didn't you see the way she looked at Caitlin?"

Phyllis blinked rapidly in confusion. Every once in a while Alice came back from her battlefield and said something vaguely coherent.

"Here she comes!" Isabel leaned against the door frame.

Caitlin entered Sophie's room and the conversation stopped. "What are you girls up to?"

"Nothing," they replied in unison. Caitlin looked at each one in turn.

Phyllis relented. "All right." The others tried to hush her but she held up her hand. "We were discussing what to get you for your birthday."

"We were? I thought we were discussing—"

"Never mind, Alice." Sophie butted in. "What Phyll said." The others nodded in agreement.

"Don't worry about that."

"Can we at least get a birthday cake? I like cake." Alice said.

"I'll see what I can do." Caitlin walked out, shaking her head.

"That was close," Isabel whispered.

"So what do we do? We've only got two weeks left."

"We have to make sure that the doc visits often, you got me? Start getting sick."

"For real?" Isabel was horrified.

"No, you dummy! Pretend sick. We want her here to spend time with Caitlin, not sticking us with needles."

"And if it comes to that?" Sophie asked.

"Hmmm." Phyllis thought for a moment. "Is it worth getting hurt? I suppose not. If it comes to that, just fess up."

"Who's first?" Sophie certainly hoped it wasn't her. "I've already had my turn."

"You could have a relapse."

"And have her poking around my ass? Not that it's an unpleasant idea if she's doing it, but if I have no hope of reeling this puppy in I'm not sure my ass is ready to donate to the cause."

"I will."

Phyllis looked at Doris standing in the doorway. "I thought you'd made your mind up to go home."

"I said that I was thinking about it."

"Well, don't take too long or you'll miss out on all the fun."

"I think I already have." Doris moved in and propped herself on the end of Sophie's bed. "I'm coming to realize that at our age we have to stick together."

"Yeah? What made you decide that?" Sophie shifted her feet.

"I haven't seen my daughter since I arrived."

Phyllis studied Doris and couldn't help but notice the sad look. "Maybe she was giving you a chance to try out this place without interference."

"Could be, but she could at least call and say hello."

"She might not have our number."

"But she has Dr. Stokes' number."

"Hey," Isabel sidled up to Doris and sat next to her. She slipped her arm around Doris's shoulders. "It's only a few days. She'll visit lots of times, won't she?"

"Err, yeah... sure." Phyllis said uncertainly. The telephone rang loudly.

"See? I bet that's her now." Isabel said.

"Doris! Phone!" Caitlin called.

"See?" Phyllis helped her up and pushed her out the door. "Okay, Alice—"

"Yes, Sergeant." Alice stood at attention and Phyllis rolled her eyes.

"You will have the runs."

"And where do you want me to run to?"

Alice was gone again. "Never mind," Phyllis said. "Isabel, you have the runs."

"Do I have to? I think I'd like a fainting spell, preferably onto my bed."

"That'd look suspicious. C'mon, we have to make this look real."

"Do I have to eat something nasty to have the runs?"

"No, a fake one will suffice."

Sophie shook her head. "She'll never fall for that, especially if there isn't any evidence, so to speak."

"Oh, there'll be evidence."

Sophie, Isabel and Alice looked at one another then screwed up their faces. "Ewww!"

Doris returned from her phone call. She didn't look too happy, Phyllis thought.

"Bad news?"

"My daughter said she'll pick me up in the morning. Early."

"And so it starts…," Sophie muttered.

"What?" Doris looked from Sophie to Phyllis.

"Just ignore her. Her asteroids are acting up."

"Maybe you should get Dr. Stokes to see her."

"It's probably a little early to do that now. Let's give her a couple of days."

"If she pokes anything but her finger at me, I'm coming after you!" Sophie threatened.

Chapter Eleven

The Woman Who Cried Wolf

"I don't like her," Phyllis whispered out the side of her mouth.

Sandra stood in the hallway, glaring at them. "Come on, mother. What's holding you up?"

"No, not at all," Phyllis continued.

Doris looked back in Sophie's room to check she had packed everything. "If it's all right with you, Caitlin, I'll leave my things here and arrange for my other belongings to be moved."

"For now, let's keep everything together." Sandra went into the room and collected a small overnight bag she had left behind.

"But, dear—"

"Come on, mother. Time's wasting." Sandra placed her hand on her mother's back and pushed her toward the front door.

"What's the hurry?"

"Nothing, but I've got things to do."

"Excuse me," Caitlin interceded. "Doris, have you decided to stay?"

"Yes dear. Sandra will organize for my things to come this week. Is that all right?"

"Certainly. We look forward to your arrival. It has been a pleasure."

"Something's going on." Phyllis muttered.

"Do you want me to eliminate her?" Alice answered.

"No!" Phyllis said a little too loudly, attracting the attention of Sandra and Caitlin. She smiled back at them and waved her hand. Phyllis glanced at Doris and smirked, pleased to see a glimmer of happiness in her eyes. "See you soon."

Doris nodded and smiled.

"Are you sure you wouldn't like to have a coffee before you leave?"

"The doc was right. You do have a fixation on coffee," Isabel commented.

"Sorry. I do that when I'm nervous."

"Thank you for taking the time—"

"Time to go." Sandra cut Doris off and continued to nudge her toward the door.

"Stop pushing!"

"You've had your chance to say goodbye, now let's go." Sandra reached for the handle and opened the door. Once Doris was out of the house, Sandra turned and faced them all. "Well… yeah."

And they were gone.

"Not even a 'thank you'." Sophie mumbled.

"What a bitch!" Isabel said, drawing a surprised look from Caitlin. "What?"

"I think we can forgive her one little expletive," Sophie said.

"It's not that. I didn't even know you knew the word."

"Ahh, Caitlin, my dear, I know lots of words." Isabel turned on her heel and walked back to her crosswords.

"So what do you think?" Phyllis asked.

"What do I think?" Caitlin repeated. "I think that may be the last we see of dear old Doris."

"Yeah," Phyllis grumbled before she turned to leave. "That's what I'm afraid of."

†

The house creaked as the coolness of the night air settled. It was an eerie noise, and one that was not often heard by the residents inside. Except this night the quiet shuffle of feet accompanied the lonely sound. The back door clicked as the lock was released and the door squeaked open. The screen door added its own melody to the building symphony as it moved and the black clad figure crept outside.

With shovel and bucket in hand, the figure approached the side fence and began to dig. The shovel scraped against the dirt and drew the attention of the dog next door. It snuffled around the fence as the digging continued.

Finally, the digging stopped. "Screw this," the figure said roughly. She dropped the shovel and carried the bucket to the side gate and out the front of the property, before creeping down the driveway of next door.

The dog growled ominously, but this didn't deter the intruder. "It's time, you traitor!"

At the sound of the words, the dog whimpered and took off to the back fence, cowering under a bush. The gate opened and the figure nimbly passed through, closing the gate silently. "Now," she whispered to herself, "to the mission."

The dog lay quietly in the hope of being missed, but his luck ran out. The small figure swept aside the bush and glared at him. "I need something from you...."

†

"What is that god-awful smell?"

Phyllis tracked the odor to the bathroom. More specifically to a bucket sitting in the corner of said room. "Alice!"

"Stop yelling!" Caitlin called.

"Get your wrinkly butt in here!"

"What's all this yelling about?" Caitlin stopped dead and sniffed. "Oh God, what is that smell?"

"I think it's coming from there." Phyllis pointed at the offending bucket. "Alice!"

"Stop...!" Caitlin sighed and dropped her volume. "Stop yelling," she spoke quietly.

"Captain. It's good to see you." Alice stood at attention and saluted.

"What is that?" Caitlin now pointed at the bucket.

"It's top secret."

"For who?"

Alice's gaze slipped to Phyllis.

"Why are you looking at me?"

80

"You should know better than to suggest something in front of her," Caitlin muttered.

"That order was cancelled, soldier."

"What are you up to?"

"You don't want to know."

"Oh yes, I do. If it involves all of you, I most certainly want to know." Caitlin turned to Alice. "What were your orders?"

"To obtain waste from the enemy."

"You made her go get dog poop?"

"It was a passing thought."

"One that Alice felt needed fulfilling." There was a pounding on the front door. "No need to guess who that is. Alice, get rid of that outside. Phyllis, don't move. I want to have a talk with you." Caitlin left the two women to answer the door.

Caitlin shook her head as she made her way to the front door. "Unbelievable..." The pounding started up again. "Coming!" she called. Reluctantly, she opened the door to find an angry next door neighbor. "Barbara."

"You promised me that you would keep that woman out of my backyard and away from my dog."

"Good to see you. How are you this morning?"

"Your humor is not appreciated. We'd just gotten Rex's limp fixed and now this."

"Why, what happened?" But she knew. Alice happened.

"The dog is scooting around the backyard on his ass."

"I thought that was normal."

"For the last four hours? He cringes and pees when the toddler comes near him. We'll probably have to take him to a psychiatrist." Barbara sighed, as if tired. "Why Caitlin? Why not Martha's Maltese, Pixie, on the other side of you? Why us?"

"It's probably because Rex is a German shepherd. I'm so sorry, Barbara. I'll take care of it. It won't happen again."

Barbara turned away and walked down the ramp. "Don't make promises you can't keep."

"Alice!" Caitlin yelled, instantly forgetting her directive from moments before.

"She's outside," Phyllis yelled back.

"Outside… oh Lord." Caitlin ran out onto the back patio just as Alice dumped the bucket load of shit over the fence into Barbara's backyard. She was about to yell but decided against it. The noise would only attract Barbara's attention, not that the pile of shit against the fence wouldn't do the same thing.

"Mission accomplished, Captain." Alice smiled as she saluted. "I have returned the contents to the owner."

"What was that for?" Caitlin pointed at the shovel and the hole.

"I tried tunneling under the fence but this old, tired body just couldn't manage it."

Caitlin seriously doubted that Alice didn't have the energy. After all, this was the same woman who threw herself out a bedroom window to wrestle a visiting cat to the ground. It was more like impatience or laziness that made her give up so easily.

Alice reached for the shovel.

"Give it here." Caitlin took it and began to fill in the hole. "Don't do this again, especially if Phyllis tells you to."

"The sergeant? Is she a spy?"

"No!" Caitlin said. The last thing she wanted was Alice trying to jump the woman at every opportunity. "It's just… just…" It was a dangerous thing to be thinking on one's feet, and Caitlin could already feel her size eight shoe slipping into her mouth. "Her plans have not been approved by Bomber Command yet." Caitlin smiled. Maybe this spontaneity thing wasn't so bad.

"Then I will ready myself for the orders to invade."

"No! Oh Hell no! No invasion, Alice. We're winning the war on another front. Our orders are to hold this line. You got me? No invasion." Caitlin felt her pulse rate go up. What had she done?

†

Thursday came around but there was no contact from Doris or Sandra. Phyllis decided that she needed to take matters into her own hands.

"Alice!" she hollered.

"Phyllis! Stop yelling!" Caitlin yelled back.

"Yes, sergeant?"

"I don't think Sophie is well. Go tell Caitlin to call the doctor."

"We have a medic?"

"She doubles as the major, Corporal. Now go do your duty."

Alice saluted and trotted out the back door to the garden to find her superior. "Captain, one of the troops is in need of medical assistance."

"Who is it? It's not serious, is it?"

"Sophie's asteroids are acting up. We need the medic."

"Again? She's not going to like this."

"Nevertheless, Captain, that is what has been reported from the front."

"Fine, tell your fellow soldiers I'll give her a call." Caitlin watched Alice trot up the path to the back door. "Something's up."

Chapter Twelve

Undone

Phyllis was happy. The doc was with Sophie and would be soon available for some careful interrogation.

"Phyllis!"

She heard Sophie's howl. So the doc had indeed used something besides her finger. She now had two angry women to contend with.

Mel came out the back door and glared at Phyllis.

"Oh-oh," Phyllis mumbled. "Is there a problem?"

"I don't know. You tell me."

"Sophie wasn't happy? You lost your charm or something?"

"That part was fine. I couldn't find a thing wrong with Sophie. Why am I here?"

"We were just doing what she asked, Doc. She complained that it hurt to go to the bathroom."

"She didn't say that."

"Hmmm, must have slipped her mind."

"How could something like that slip your mind? She's got asteroids, for heaven's sake!"

"Hemorrhoids," Phyllis corrected.

"Asteroids, hemorrhoids, I don't care what part of the constellation they come from. The point is that she seems perfectly fine and she called out your name. You're up to something."

"I swear, Doc, I didn't make the call."

"I've got better things to do with my time than come out here for a false alarm. Have you ever heard of the boy who cried wolf?"

"Wasn't he eaten?"

"That was because he cried once too often. Don't you do the same." Mel opened the screen door forcefully and disappeared inside.

Alice stepped out and looked at her. "You told me to tell Caitlin."

"Yes, I did, but I distinctly remember *not* making that call."

†

"That was strange."

Caitlin looked up from her kneading when Mel walked into the kitchen. "What was strange?"

"Sophie. I just examined her and I couldn't find anything wrong."

"Maybe she wanted to see you again."

"You think so?"

"I wouldn't think she'd waste your time, but who knows?" Caitlin moved to the sink and washed her hands. "Coffee?"

"Just a quick one. I have an appointment back at the center."

Caitlin placed the kettle on the stove. "Have you had lunch?"

"I'll get something on my way back to work."

"Nonsense." She grabbed the loaf of bread. "I haven't got much for filling. Grape jelly or peanut butter?"

Mel laughed. "I haven't had a peanut butter and jelly sandwich since I was a kid."

"Then peanut butter and jelly it is." She prepared some sandwiches, making enough to feed them both. By the time she finished the water had boiled. "There you go." She placed down the plate of sandwiches and followed quickly with two mugs of coffee.

"I don't know how you do it," Mel said.

"Do what?" Caitlin sat down opposite Mel.

"Cope with all of this." Mel waved her hand in a wide arc. "The women and the housework, with no obvious time for yourself. It's a lot to take on."

"I don't mind. It's nice to know that I make a difference, even it's only a small one."

Mel reached for a sandwich. "Don't belittle what you do. It's not a small one. These women rely on you to keep them safe and well. Not everyone would be so generous. It must play havoc with your love life."

"Love life?"

"Sorry, forget I said that." Mel glanced at Caitlin for a moment before returning her attention to the sandwich in her hand.

"Why do you want to know?"

"No reason." Mel lifted the sandwich and took a bite before she said anything more. She took her time chewing the food in her mouth and studied Caitlin silently. After she swallowed she spoke, "I just think that everyone should be happy. Is that a crime?"

"Not in my book. For now, however, these women are my life. That may change in the future, I don't know, but I can't let it interfere with my work."

"It sounds lonely." Mel took another bite.

Caitlin reached for a sandwich. "Most of the time it doesn't worry me."

"But there are other times."

"Late at night... well, let's just say a pillow doesn't keep you warm at night."

"You're just not holding it right."

Caitlin laughed then took another bite of her sandwich.

Phyllis stood in the doorway. "Doc, can I talk to you?"

Mel looked at Caitlin then at Phyllis. "Come and sit down. Do you want Caitlin to leave?"

"No, it doesn't bother me. It," she stopped and took a deep breath, "it's about Doris. We haven't heard a thing since she left. Has she changed her mind?"

"Not that I know of. You haven't heard anything? That's strange."

"Well, that daughter of hers was a bit snippy. She couldn't wait to get her out of this place."

"That's Sandra, all right. I don't know what I can do though. I've probably overstepped my bounds as it is."

"Could you check with her and see she's okay?"

"Why do you care?" Mel looked into Phyllis's eyes. "Taken an interest in her, have you?"

"No! Of course not!" Phyllis said the words a little too harshly.

"Right."

"It's not like that."

"You do realize she's straight," Caitlin said.

"You two are impossible!" Phyllis let out a grunt and left.

Mel laughed quietly and waited a few moments before speaking. "So, what do you think? Has Phyllis got a case of a schoolgirl crush?"

"Hard to tell. Doris was a nice lady and she and Phyllis seemed to hit it off, in a non-sexual sort of way. They spent a lot of time talking. Maybe she's just missing someone new to talk to."

"Could be, but it's not as much fun to tease her with."

Caitlin glared at her.

"What?" Mel let the sandwich dangle close to her mouth. "She's zinged me a few times in the past few weeks. Turn around is fair play."

"No wonder you don't have a girlfriend."

"I'm in between engagements at the moment."

"You were engaged? You do that often?"

"Engagements as in... ahh, never mind. I'm in between girlfriends."

"No wonder, if you fling around engagements like they're M & M's. You are a sad, sad woman."

Mel leaned back and let her head drop. "You are impossible, Caitlin."

Caitlin smiled. "Difficult but not impossible, Dr. Stokes."

Mel stopped. Was that what she was hoping to hear? Did Caitlin leave the door slightly ajar for her? Caitlin's face showed no hint of invitation and the moment slipped by. "I better get back. Can you tell your ladies not to make any more hoax calls? I have a pretty heavy schedule this week."

"Sure."

"In the meantime, I'll call Doris and see what's going on."

"Okay."

"I'm sorry to eat and run, but—"

87

"No need to apologize. I'm sorry about Sophie."

Mel stood and walked to the front door, closely followed by Caitlin. "You take care."

"You too."

Phyllis appeared in the hallway on her way to the back door.

"Phyllis?" Mel called. "Can I talk to you for a minute? Outside." She tilted her head toward the front door.

"I didn't do anything," Phyllis said as she lifted herself out of her wheelchair and walked down the ramp to the driveway.

Mel waited for the door to close before she began. "I'm sorry for snapping at you before. It was very unprofessional."

"Are you going to give up on Caitlin so easily?"

"I… ahh…" What could she say? The question was bold and unexpected, just like Phyllis. "What business is it of yours?"

"You're not doing such a good job, Doc. Someone has to step in."

"I've given her all the subtle clues I can. She's doesn't have the time or the commitment to date."

"Aww, she's just saying that."

"Well, in case you didn't notice, that's all I can go on. I've all but said 'go out with me' and she indicated 'no'."

"No, you have joked about it. She doesn't know if you're serious or not." Phyllis leaned against the Chevy's hood. "Just grab the girl and kiss her."

Mel sighed and her gaze dropped to the ground. "It's not that simple."

"It is that simple, Doc."

"I tell you what. The next opportunity I get I'll broach the subject with her."

"It still sounds like you're chickening out, Doc."

"I will, if you stop calling in bogus illnesses. Deal?"

"I dunno. We were enjoying your visits."

"I'm getting too old for this shit," Mel muttered.

"Walk a mile in my shoes," Phyllis replied. "All right deal, but if you slack off all bets are off."

Mel didn't know what to say next so she left the conversation at that. She nodded goodbye and walked toward her car. While she was glad to see Caitlin, the constant travelling to and fro was wearing her out. As much as she enjoyed the visits it had to stop.

†

"Everyone in here, now!" Caitlin's voice boomed through the house.

"Uh, oh," Sophie mumbled.

"You called?" Phyllis said innocently.

"Sit!" Caitlin stared at them, one at a time, showing them her displeasure. "Just what did you think you were doing?"

"We didn't do anything."

"You did plenty. Don't deny it."

"But, Captain—"

"Alice, shut up!"

Isabel's eyes grew wide.

"Now, hang on—" Phyllis started.

"No, you hang on. You caused a lot of trouble. This is no game. What if you kept Dr. Stokes from an emergency, like a heart attack? Do you want that person's death on your conscience?"

"But it didn't happen, so what's the beef?"

"The beef as you call it, Phyllis, is that it was an unnecessary trip for the doctor. You pulled her away from her practice and now she has to go back and try to catch up on the hour or so you took up carrying out this little prank. You heard the story of the boy who cried wolf?"

Phyllis smiled.

"And what's so funny?"

"The doc and I talked about that half an hour ago."

"And did you take any notice?"

"I knew what she was talking about."

"I... I..." Caitlin was speechless. "Get out of my sight!"

The women were slow to move back to their rooms. Isabel looked over her shoulder at Caitlin, who waved her off.

"I'll call you when dinner is ready."

Caitlin sat down. She'd never spoken to them like that before and it unnerved her. Then again, she'd never been given a reason to do so before. While at times they could be unruly, they'd never actively involved outsiders in their pranks. Caitlin overlooked their tomfoolery, but to involve the doc and possibly put someone at risk, well that was crossing the line. A headache reared its ugly head and Caitlin retired to her bedroom to rest.

✝

"Wow!" Isabel said, "I've never seen her that angry."

"She'll be fine in an hour or two," Phyllis said confidently.

"What do we do now?"

"We could try again, but I think Caitlin has had enough."

"That's probably the best," Isabel agreed.

"Of course, there's still Doris to sort out, so we may get lucky."

"Lucky?" Sophie asked. "Why will it be lucky for us? This is for Caitlin's benefit, not ours."

"And if she's happy, we're happy. Right?"

"And who will look after us while she's off getting a life?"

"Shame on you for thinking of yourselves like that. She deserves something more than this." The women looked at Phyllis. "All right. There may be a little inconvenience for us, but she shouldn't have to suffer for it."

"So, we're back where we started," Sophie said.

"Not quite," Phyllis grinned.

Chapter Thirteen

A New Direction

Mel stood outside Doris's front door. A phone call could have answered her question for her, but she decided she needed to look into Doris's eyes when she talked to her. She pressed the doorbell.

"Yes? Who is it?"

"Doris, its Dr. Stokes." Mel waited for the door to open. Doris looked at her sheepishly. "I was surprised you didn't call." There was a moment of silence. "Can I come in?"

Doris stood aside and let her enter. She closed the door quietly and walked into the living room, waiting for Mel to take a seat.

Mel made herself comfortable. "Is everything okay?"

"Everything is fine."

But Mel knew it wasn't. She could see it in Doris's eyes and in her posture. Sandra had gotten to her and she didn't want to have this conversation. "Is it... really?"

"I'm fine, Dr. Stokes. I think I'll stay here a little while longer."

"That's a shame." She could feel the sting of defeat, and it annoyed her that Sandra had won. "Phyllis was asking after you."

"Really?"

"She wanted to make sure you were all right." *Bad Mel*, she thought. "I think she missed her friend." Doris's head bobbed along with the conversation. "I thought you two were getting along."

"We are. I mean we did."

"Then, why are you here?"

"Sandra thought it best I hold on here a little longer. She said I wasn't ready for that sort of thing."

That's not what she told me. What are you playing at, Sandra?
"Did you enjoy your time at Shady Oakes?"

"It was lovely."

"So, that's it then. You're going to give up a chance of friendship and healthy conversation to stay here?"

"Yes. No. I don't know. I'm so confused." Mel could hear Doris's distress and she knew Doris was trying to appease both of them.

"Let's just say for a moment that neither Sandra nor I were around to influence you. What would you do?"

Doris looked at Mel sadly.

"Be honest. If you didn't have to keep either of us happy, where would you stay?"

"I'm afraid to lose his memory."

Mel stood up and moved to Doris. "He doesn't reside here." Mel swept her arm around the room. "He resides here." She let her palm hover over Doris's heart, mindful not to touch her. "His memory will be with you wherever you are."

†

Phyllis and Sophie clustered around the computer at the local library as Isabel called up the search engine. "What was the daughter's name again?"

"Sandra something," Sophie muttered.

"Boyer... I think that's what the doc said." Phyllis waited impatiently while Isabel typed in the name.

"This is going to take a while. Why don't you go find a book or something?"

"How long is a while?" Phyllis started to nibble on a fingernail. When she realized what she was doing she pulled her hand away abruptly.

"I don't know. It takes as long as it takes."

"Well, hurry up. We don't have all day." Phyllis pushed away her chair and wheeled off in the direction of the fiction section. Her chair was not ideal, and she had to put up with the wobble when the dent in the wheel hit the floor, but until the new wheelchair arrived it was all she had. She rolled slowly along the rows of books, instantly dismissing most of them. A librarian blocked her way as he stacked books on the shelves.

"Excuse me. Do you have any lesbian literature?"

He glanced at her with what she would have described as disdain. "I don't think so. Let me check." He backed away smoothly and walked to his desk.

"Pinhead," Phyllis muttered. She continued her lazy, bumpy roll along the aisle looking at the shelves for something of interest.

He returned moments later. "Sorry, no."

"That's rather short-sighted, don't you think?"

He huffed at her and returned to the stocking of books.

She moved from that aisle quickly after his hostile gaze met her every time she looked. Maybe fiction wasn't her 'thing'. Phyllis steered her battered wheelchair to the other side of the building and proceeded to look at the books sitting there. One section caught her eye.

Phyllis slowed her meandering to a stop and studied the titles sitting there. She'd never really been interested in hobbies before. Maybe it was time to give it a go. Painting? *Hmmm, maybe*. Knitting. *Hell, no!* Embroidery. *Kill me now!* Woodwork, *Not really*. However there were a handful of books on woodcarving. There had been some really nice pieces around when she was traveling on her bike and she'd often wondered what it would be like to do something like that. She gave it some thought before reaching up and taking two books from the shelf. After all, it didn't cost anything to read about it.

Phyllis returned to Isabel. "You've had enough time. What have you found?"

Isabel looked at her in shock. "It's going to take a lot longer than this to get anywhere."

"I thought you said you were a wiz with this sort of thing."

"I said a wiz, not a miracle worker."

"A miracle worker?" Caitlin had joined them at the computer.

"Nothing. She wants me to find something."

"She's taking too long."

"Maybe I can help."

"No!" Phyllis said forcefully. "No, Isabel can manage. Can't you, dear?"

Isabel blinked. "Dear? You've never called—"

"Never mind that," Phyllis cut her off. "Just keep looking." She turned her wheelchair to face Caitlin. "Where's Sophie? Or, more to the point, where's Alice?"

"Alice is looking at what she calls picture books."

"Huh?"

"Photos from World War II. She seemed engrossed in it so I took the opportunity to see what the rest of you were up to." Caitlin glanced at the books tucked down beside Phyllis's legs. "I see you've found something."

"Yeah." She pulled the books out for Caitlin to see. "Thought I'd have a look to see what was involved."

"You know, we can do something about that now."

Phyllis smiled. "Yeah." She studied Caitlin and saw the tense lines around her eyes had eased. "We have a little breathing space."

"It sure was welcome. But there's no point counting your chickens before they hatch. I want to make sure the money is in my hot little hand before I go spending any of it."

"Have you decided yet?"

"Since it's for all of us, I thought about getting some things for the house, like maybe some more games." Caitlin's gaze dropped to the books at Phyllis's side. "Or hobbies."

"That'd be great. We might be able to finally keep Alice occupied."

"Hmm. Maybe we should buy a jungle gym."

Phyllis laughed. "How about a parachute? Or maybe a zip line?"

"Oh, please! Don't give her more reasons to try and break her neck."

Still the image of Alice's spindly legs flailing about as she barreled down a zip line attached to the roof brought a smile to Phyllis's lips.

"Could we get some lesbian fiction? This library doesn't have any."

"Sure, I can't see why not. You're not interested in regular fiction?"

"Please! Who wants to read about some guy nailing a chick? He's got no idea what he's doing."

Caitlin laughed. "Sure he does. Remember, it's what is considered the 'norm' in society these days."

"What do they know? In my book, the 'norm' in being with the one you love, no matter which sex he or she is."

"Touché."

"And it's a shame that there are so many ignorant bastards out there in the world who don't realize that."

Caitlin looked at her thoughtfully.

"What?"

"Maybe you should run for office."

"Hell, no! Why would I want to complicate my life surrounded by ignorant bigots?"

"You're right. How stupid of me." Caitlin chuckled softly. She looked around the room "Where's Sophie?"

"Try the magazines."

"Ahh." As Phyllis spoke Sophie appeared with an armful of magazines.

"Woo hoo!" she cried, drawing the sound of *shhh* from nearby visitors. "Sorry. Woo hoo!" she repeated softly.

"What have you got there?" Caitlin asked.

"Got me some new pictures to look at." Sophie gleefully hugged the magazines to her chest.

"They're not going to let you take that many home."

"No?' Awww." Sophie pulled the magazines away from her chest and looked at them sadly. "That means I gotta choose?"

"Sure do."

"How many?"

"I don't know. Let me check." Caitlin wandered off to the librarian's desk.

"What do you want them for?" Phyllis grumbled.

"Have you seen the women in here? They're gorgeous."

"And not available. Why bother?"

"You know, Phyllis, you have no romance in your soul. I may be old, but I'm not dead."

"You need to get a hobby."

"And I don't see you doing anything either."

"If you're so intent on women, why not draw them or something?"

"Oooh, that sounds interesting. It'd nearly be like sliding my hands across them, wouldn't it?"

Phyllis shivered. "You are a sick, sick woman."

"Tracing every contour."

"Sophie," Phyllis warned. Sophie closed her eyes and smiled. "Don't make me hurt you."

Phyllis caught a glimpse of Isabel writing something down. She left Sophie to daydream. "What did you find?"

"I have a name and address."

"Of who? Where she works? Bank details?"

"Sandra's name and address."

"And that's it?"

"I told you it would take time. Don't rush me."

"So, in six months' time you can tell me she drives a Ford pickup?"

"Does she? I can cross that off the list."

"I don't care what she friggin' drives!" The sound of hissing made Phyllis drop her voice. "I want to know what has her all fired up about keeping Doris at home. From what Doris said, she doesn't visit, so there must be something else about that house that has her interest."

Caitlin returned with Alice in tow. "Time to go, girls. Have you got all the reading material you want?"

Sophie was seated as she sorted through her pile of magazines. "Only four, Sophie."

"Four?" Sophie said plaintively. "Damn!" She glanced up to see Caitlin's look of disapproval. "Sorry. Now, let me see...." She took her time sorting through each magazine, taking a few minutes to decide on the four she would ultimately take. Finally satisfied with her choices, although disappointed to leave the others behind, she joined the group to have their books scanned.

Chapter Fourteen

The Whole Truth

When they arrived home there was a black sedan parked outside on the street. Caitlin glanced at it now and then as she helped her charges inside. Suddenly the driver's side door opened.

"Caitlin!" Sandra called.

"Sandra, nice to see you." She didn't really mean it. In fact, she disliked the woman who seemed, to her, to take enjoyment in bossing her mother around.

Sandra slipped around to the passenger door and opened it. She lent a hand to Doris to help her out.

"Doris! Are you here for a visit?"

"No, I'm here to stay," she announced cheerfully.

Caitlin's eyebrows rose and she glanced at Sandra. The woman looked impassively back at her and Caitlin wondered what was going on in her head.

"That's great news! Come in!" Caitlin extended her hand and allowed Doris to pass by. She watched Sandra go to the trunk of her car and lift out a large suitcase. She retrieved another, smaller bag and walked toward the house, leaving the heavier suitcase sitting on the grass.

"You don't mind, do you?" Sandra said smoothly and Caitlin felt herself react.

"Of course not." She paused for a moment to watch Sandra walk to the front door before she grabbed the bag. "Vindictive bit... No, that's not charitable," Caitlin mumbled. With a sigh she followed Sandra inside the home.

†

"What's she doing here?" Phyllis said.

"I thought you said she wanted to keep Doris home?" Sophie asked.

"That's what I thought. I wonder what she's up to?"

"Maybe you were wrong." Isabel suggested.

The women crowded around the front door to watch the interaction between Caitlin and Sandra.

"That answers the question what type of car she drives. Do you want me to stop the investigation?"

"No, I'm not convinced yet."

"But—"

"There's something about Doris's home that has Sandra's interest. I want to know what it is."

"It's really none of your business, you know." Alice piped in.

"Haven't you ever had a feeling something was wrong?"

"Yeah," Alice replied. "It involved green peppers and a burrito." Phyllis scowled at her. "Why don't you ask Doris?"

Phyllis blinked. "You know, Alice, that's not a bad idea." Now all she needed to do was to cover the question in a lot of bullshit to avoid detection.

"Hello, everyone," Doris announced.

"Good to see you back," Isabel replied before she turned and made her way to her room. Alice saluted her and did an about turn, marching off in a military style to the dining room table. She sat down with a pack of cards and proceeded to shuffle them with a surprising amount of manual dexterity. Sophie giggled and trundled down the hallway with the magazines under her arm.

"Guess that leaves you and me." Phyllis said quietly.

"Here's your bag. I'll arrange for the rest of your things to be delivered soon." Sandra stood aside as Caitlin struggled in with the bag. "What will she need?"

"Give me a moment," Caitlin huffed. She found a pen and paper and made a small list. "This is probably all she needs, at least for now. She can make arrangements later about her home and what could go into storage."

"Fine." Sandra snatched the paper and walked to her mother to plant a peck on her cheek. "You be good." Before Caitlin had a chance to get some emergency contact details Sandra was gone.

"O-kay." Caitlin stood there stunned. "I guess I'll have to get her details from you. In the meantime, let's get you settled." Caitlin picked up the large bag and nearly dragged it down the hallway. "You can take my room until your bed arrives."

"And where will you sleep?"

"Don't worry about that. It'll only be for a few days... I hope."

Finally Doris and Phyllis were alone. "You were worried about me." Doris stated rather than asked.

"Errr, yeah." Phyllis couldn't look her in the eye.

"Why?"

"Well, you said you'd come back and then you didn't." Phyllis shifted in her wheelchair. "I wasn't worried one way or the other. I just wanted to make sure that you hadn't had a fall or something. No skin off my nose." She rolled the chair toward the back door.

Doris walked after her. "No, I don't accept that." She moved around the wheelchair and opened the screen door for her. "You could have called Dr. Stokes."

Phyllis remained silent.

"You were the one who told her."

"As I said, I was just making sure you were okay."

Doris took a seat on the bench.

"You changed your mind... again. Staying this time?"

Doris looked out over the backyard and the vegetable patch. "Seems so."

"You're not sure? Geez, woman, make up your mind!"

"No, I'm staying."

"Maybe I should get your address in case you decide to make your escape." Phyllis glanced quickly at the woman seated beside her. "Can't let you off that easily."

Doris remained quiet for a moment. "I'll make you a deal."

Phyllis's defences went up. "What sort of deal?" She eyed her suspiciously.

"I'll tell you anything you want to know, but you have to tell me about Stonewall."

"There's nothing to tell." Phyllis said grumpily.

"Oh, but I think there is. Something that has you tied up in knots. What could possibly be so bad that you have had it bottled up inside you all these years? Did you kill someone?"

"You've been here less than a minute and you want to know my life story?"

"Fine," Doris said. "So it's okay to know my story but not yours, eh? Guess I'll just have to remain a mystery to you."

"That's hardly fair. All I'm asking for is your address. You want a whole lot more." Doris continued to look out over the backyard. "Aww, come on. It's in the past. Why drag it up now?" Doris stood and reached for the back door. "Wait!" Doris looked at her and smiled. Phyllis sighed in defeat. "If you tell anyone I will kill you. I will find you and run you over with my wheelchair... several times. By the time I've finished with you you'll look like road kill. If you—"

"All right already! I get the point." Doris sat down again and folded her arms.

"What do you want to know?" Phyllis felt her chest tighten.

"Firstly—"

Phyllis's head dropped. There was going to be more than one question.

"What's Stonewall?"

"If you were a lesbian you wouldn't be asking." Phyllis sighed. "You got to remember that in the Fifties and Sixties it was downright ugly to be gay. If there was even a whiff of you being homosexual you were, at best, thrown in jail or, at worst, sent to a psychiatric hospital to get 'readjusted'. I'd been locked up in prison once before and I didn't want that to happen again."

"Stonewall Inn was a bar in the Village in New York. It was like any other dive that catered to the gays at that time. They'd regularly be rumbled by the cops and shut down, only to open again a few days later."

"What was so special about this place?"

"Special? Nothing really. Except in June 1969 it was a matter of being in the wrong place at the wrong time for some. The cops did their usual early morning raid, except this time they got more than they bargained for. The paddy wagons were slow to respond and a crowd had gathered to watch the fun. There was pushing and shoving and the police found themselves outnumbered. The gays finally found some balls and pushed back."

"And where are you in this story?"

Phyllis looked at her hands and saw the slight tremor. "I was in that crowd."

"And you pushed back?"

"No," Phyllis said quietly. "I ran." When Doris remained silent, Phyllis continued. "I was a coward. I'd revealed myself once before and was thrown out by my family. I couldn't do that again. I'm no hero, Doris, despite whatever Sophie thinks. I'm a liar and a coward."

"You're too harsh on yourself."

"I'm a fake. I've spent most of my life running from that fraudster. After a while I realized that I'd never escape, so I tried to find some peace with myself. Now, you've brought that all up again."

"No, you've never let it go otherwise you wouldn't be fighting to keep it secret."

"I'm so tired of it."

"Then drop it."

"It's not as easy as that."

"It **is** as easy as that." Doris reached and put her hand on Phyllis's. "It's in the past and you can't change it. Let it go."

Phyllis looked into Doris's eyes. "I don't know if I can. It's been a part of me for so long. I… I'll try."

"That's all you can do." Doris withdrew her hand.

Phyllis closed her eyes for a moment then opened them to gaze at the vegetable garden. "Now, what's your address?"

"I'll write it down for you."

"Are you trying to get out of our deal?"

"Do you see pen and paper anywhere?"

"Why was Sandra trying to stop you from coming here?"

"She said because it was one of 'those places'. She may be a bigot but she's still my daughter."

"What made her change her mind?"

"I put my foot down and said I was going."

Phyllis seriously doubted that. To her, Sandra was well in control of her mother and would only let her go if it was to her advantage. "Does Sandra have some sort of stake in your house?"

Doris stared at her. "Why do you want to know?"

"I'm making sure I understand Sandra and her motives."

"She doesn't have any motives," Doris said sharply. "Or maybe you're trying to find out what the house is worth to you."

"No, that's not it at all."

"I don't like where this conversation is going."

"Doris, I'm not interested in your damned house."

"Yes you are, otherwise why are you asking such a personal question?"

"Because I want to know what Sandra's interest is in your house."

"She'll inherit it, so what's the point?"

"Maybe she needs the money sooner than later."

"That's a horrible thing to say!"

"Just answer the question!"

"No."

"We made a deal."

"Fine. My house is collateral on a loan of hers. Are you happy now?"

"There have been no hassles with the loan?"

"No." Doris's eyebrows dropped ominously. "Wait. There was a message from the bank on the answering machine a few weeks ago."

"I think it may be worthwhile returning that call, don't you think?"

"I'd need my papers for that."

"Then call the doc and ask her to pick them up for you."

"She'll want to know why I didn't ask Sandra."

"Oh," Phyllis thought for a moment. "Tell her you already asked but she said she was busy."

"That's a lie."

"Really?"

"You don't need to be sarcastic."

"It's a part of me, remember?"

"No, guilt is a part of you, not sarcasm. You came up with that all by yourself."

Phyllis smiled. She liked Doris. The woman didn't take any shit from her, and in her book she got a gold star. "Unless you tell her the whole truth, that's your only alternative."

Doris sighed. "I hate lying."

"Don't we all?"

†

"Well, hello stranger!" Caitlin was pleased to see Mel standing at her front door. "What can I do for you?"

"I'm here to see Doris."

Caitlin's brow creased in anger. "I don't believe it. I told them to stop this shit." Mel raised a finger to interrupt, but Caitlin didn't see it. "Phyllis!" she yelled. "Get your wrinkly butt out here!"

"Someone call?" Phyllis rolled her wheelchair slowly down the hallway.

"I thought I told you to stop this nonsense."

"But—"

"What are you talking about? What nonsense?"

"Who's sick this time? Isabel? Alice? Or maybe it's your new friend, *Doris*." Caitlin put emphasis on Doris's name.

"Doris isn't sick."

Mel interrupted. "Excuse me—"

"So you admit it, huh? Just for that—"

There was a shrill whistle. "Can I get a word in here? Doris called me because she wanted me to pick up some things from her home."

"Why not call Sandra?"

"It seems Sandra is busy."

"And this stuff couldn't wait?" Caitlin looked from Phyllis to Mel and back again.

"Apparently not. So, if you get her I'll be out of your hair as quickly as possible."

Caitlin looked embarrassed. "I'm so sorry. I thought—"

"It's okay," Mel said before she smiled. "It was a good excuse to come by and say hello. Can I come in?" Mel moved inside the house so Caitlin could close the door.

"Coffee?" Caitlin asked nervously.

"I think I can spare a few minutes."

Caitlin walked into the kitchen and Doris appeared in the hallway.

"Dr. Stokes. Thank you for doing this."

"You sounded a little nervous on the phone. Anything I can help you with?" Doris and Phyllis exchanged glances. "What?"

"Nothing," they both said. Doris stepped up to Mel and pressed a key into her hand. She handed over a small list of items. "Here's what I need. I've tried to be as precise as I could where to find them."

"I'll pick them up this afternoon. Will tomorrow morning be soon enough for you?"

"Thank you, Dr. Stokes. I'm sorry to barge into your weekend like this."

"Not at all."

Doris and Phyllis turned.

"Phyllis? Got your new wheelchair yet?"

"Does it look like it?"

"Just asking."

Caitlin emerged from the kitchen with two mugs and set them down on the dining room table.

"What is it with everyone today?" Mel asked.

Caitlin shrugged. "Bad hair day?" She sat down and fiddled with her mug. "How have you been?"

"Fine. Busy. And you?"

"Same ol'."

"Nothing ever changes, huh?"

"We'll I'd call Doris a change, but don't tell her that."

"Besides Doris. No… um… change on the dating front?"

"Why? Are you asking?"

Mel glanced at Caitlin to see her expression. It was non-committal. "Do you want me to organize another date for you? I have a friend or two who would be more than happy to oblige."

"I don't think so. It's too much of a chore."

"And for the right woman, would it be too much of a chore?"

"I suppose not."

"Unless you meet them you're not going to know whether she's the right one or not. So, the first date is obligatory, whether you like it or not."

"True, but by the time I get to dinner I don't have a lot of energy left. These women are sweet but they are a handful."

"It sounds like you don't want to find out."

"I suppose I'm hoping that someone will drop into my lap and I don't have to go through all the mating rituals."

"Mating rituals? Hahaha." Mel laughed long and loud.

"You know what I mean."

"Yeah, I know what you mean. You want someone to come into your life who will skip all the dinners, dances and movies and can cut straight to the relaxed state of a comfortable relationship."

"Yeah but that's not going to happen anytime soon."

Mel stood and took her mug to the sink to wash it out. "You never know." She dried her hands on the towel. "You never know."

Chapter Fifteen

Garden Trip

Mel pulled up outside Doris's house to find Sandra's sedan Mel pulled up outside Doris's house to find Sandra's sedan parked in the driveway. A medical emergency had delayed her plans to collect Doris's belongings in the afternoon, and it left her with no choice but to visit at night. She moved her car a little further up the road then adjusted the rear view mirror to watch the house. What was she doing there?

A child came out, went to the car and popped open the trunk. He reached in a pulled out a bag full of, what looked like, toys. A stuffed giraffe stuck out, held in place by the zipper on top. A moment later Sandra walked out to the car removed another bag from the trunk.

Mel chewed her lip while she thought. Should she confront Sandra about this? Surely if Doris knew she would have said something. But what if Doris didn't know? By the looks of it, Sandra was moving in.

While she contemplated her next move, the porch light went out. She would have preferred to pick up Doris's things with a minimum of fuss, but it looked like it wasn't going to happen. She was tempted to move on, but she knew Doris would want to know what was happening.

Mel scrounged around in her bag to find Doris's list and her hand rested on her phone. Should she? A wicked smile crept to her face as she thought of the possibility of being a real-life Mata Hari. Not that she would go naked to achieve her goal, but the spying aspect appealed to her greatly. What was the harm in a little adventure? And if she got caught? She couldn't answer that one.

There really wasn't a good reason for her to be snooping around outside Doris's house.

Before she had a chance to change her mind, Mel grabbed her phone and her keys and climbed out of the car. She pressed the automatic lock and cringed as the car beeped loudly.

It looked like a quiet suburban street, and at that moment it seemed even quieter. An occasional bark broke the silence as she moved stealthily toward Doris's house. She kept to the shadows while she moved closer, standing behind one darkened bush then another to close the gap to her destination.

She held her breath as a side window slid open. Voices could be heard as well as the sound of the television. It seemed Sandra and her family were making themselves right at home.

After some careful manoeuvring Mel found herself under the window. She raised her phone and waited for a loud noise from the television before she pushed the button to take a picture.

It was a nerve wracking few moments as she waited for some sort of response. When none came she inhaled deeply. Despite the odds, it looked like she had gotten away with it.

Feeling brave Mel moved to the next window and did the same, slowly making her way around the front of the house and taking photos of what she could. For good measure, she added a photo or two of the car and its contents. She quickly glanced around to see if she had attracted any attention. At that moment, a dog barked and she jumped. It was time to get out of there.

Mel crept around the garden and stepped over the thigh-high fence to the neighbor's yard. The side window closed and she squatted down, her phone tumbling from her fingers into Doris's garden on the other side of the fence. "Shit!" The word came out as a harsh whisper and Mel forced herself to cut the word off. She waited to see if her hiss had drawn any attention. A moment passed and then another. When the time seemed right, she leaned over the fence to recover her cell.

Another dog bark cut through the night and Mel jerked, just enough for her to lose her balance and fall head over heels onto Doris's rose bush.

The pain was pretty extraordinary. A thousand pinpricks sent her skin into a twitching frenzy. Mel looked up at the sky and then at the window. It wasn't going to be easy to get out of this. She was stuck upside down and pinned in place. At that moment she was glad she decided not to go down the naked route. Now she knew what it felt like to be doing a handstand while Velcro™-ed upside down to a wall.

It wasn't going to be easy, or fun, to get off the bush. A round of laughter offered her a sound barrier and she took it. She threw herself sideways and bit her lip as the thorns dug deep. A moan sat in her throat and she fought tooth and nail to keep it there. There was a muffled crack as the bush gave way to her weight and she fell to the ground.

Mel looked back at the rose bush and cursed silently. It was torn apart. Her only hope was that Sandra didn't care about the garden, at least before she had a chance to collect Doris's possessions.

Painfully, Mel reached in and grabbed her cell, mentally cursing the thing for her injuries. As soon as she moved she knew driving was going to be a problem. She imagined the back of her body, from head to toe, were full of nasty thorns, because every move was agony.

Mel forced herself to reach behind and pull away the branch. She could feel the thorns coming away from the wood and she knew most of them were still in her skin. She staggered out of the garden and down the road to her car. Somehow she couldn't bring herself to try and sit down. There was one solution with two options. She only hoped that the first option would agree to come.

Mel pushed the speed dial on her phone.

"Hello?" The familiar voice could just be heard above the background noise.

"Alex?"

"Mel? What's up?" He sounded jovial enough so maybe she could call in a favor.

"Can you come pick me up?"

"Did your car break down? Maybe you should call the AA."

"No, it's not the car. It's me."

"Oh. Can it wait?"

"Yeah, sure. That's why I called you at 10 p.m. on a Saturday night. Of course it won't wait!"

"What's the problem?"

"Come on, Alex. Just pick me up."

"What about a taxi?"

"It's either you or the Emergency Department."

"God! What happened?"

"Just get your butt over here!" She gave him the address and instructions on how to approach the street. "And don't dawdle. Please." The pain made her cranky, so she added the 'please' in the hope of appealing to his Hippocratic Oath.

Half an hour later Mel's pain threshold, and her patience, had nearly reached its end. She slumped over the hood of her car and rested there as best she could. Finally the headlights of an oncoming car spread over her like a blanket. She heard the car door open and close but she didn't open her eyes until she heard Alex's voice.

"What happened to you?"

"What does it look like?"

He peered closer. "I'd say you fell into a rose bush."

"Give the man a cookie. Can you get me back to the surgery and get them out of my back?"

"Err, sure. Yeah. Where's my brain?"

Mel was so tempted to let the remark out but she wanted his help. Insulting his brain would not be a good idea. "Can you turn off the headlights? It's giving me a headache." It didn't really but telling him it would attract the attention of the neighbors would only raise more questions.

Alex helped her to the car and they stood looking at the passenger's seat uncertainly.

"Hang on." He opened the back door and lowered the back seat into the trunk.

Mel could see what he wanted her to do but she eyed him sceptically. "Really?" She couldn't even begin to figure out how to get in without some part of her damaged torso brushing the car.

"It's not going to get any easier standing there looking at it."

Mel stared at Alex grumpily. "You want to try it first?"

He laughed. Mel crawled across the seat on her hands and knees, biting her lip as the thorn pricks in her palms stung. She backed her legs into the hole left by the back seat so that her legs rested in the trunk. She felt like an idiot, and only hoped they weren't pulled over by a cop on the way to the surgery.

"Can you grab my bag from the front seat of my car?" Mel's body jostled as she reached into her pocket for her car keys. She slumped onto the seat and could feel one or two pricks of pain down her front. Her face mashed into the seat as she relaxed. Then an odor rose up to meet her nose. "Oh, God! What is that smell?"

Alex had disappeared for several moments then returned with her handbag. He closed the door after he took his seat behind the wheel.

"There is some god-awful smell back here. Did something die?"

"The girlfriend's dog." Alex stated.

"Please don't tell me he peed on the seat."

"Okay, I won't tell you."

"This is some sort of divine punishment, isn't it?"

"I don't know. What did you actually do?"

"You wouldn't believe me if I told you."

"Well, unless you tell me it'll be a moot point."

"I dropped my cell and when I reached down to pick it up I fell over a fence."

"And onto a rose bush. Are you going to tell me why you were near a fence and a rose bush?" Alex started the engine and pulled away from the kerb.

"How long?" Mel tilted her head sideways away from the patch of material that held the dog's past indiscretion.

"How long is what? The car? Little Alex? What?"

"God!"

"Lighten up."

"You're not the one with a thorn negotiating its way up your ass."

111

Alex laughed loudly. At a stoplight, he glanced over his shoulder and laughed even harder. "You certainly made the trip worth it."

"I'm glad someone's enjoying my pain."

"Not far to go," he said, "but you may find yourself wishing to be still in the car when I start removing those little suckers."

Mel sighed. "That's what I'm afraid of."

†

"How much longer?" It was like plucking out her body hair one strand at a time.

"I've removed all the loose ones."

"The loose ones? You mean that was the easy part?"

"I'm working as fast as I can."

Mel sighed and closed her eyes. "Sorry. The pain's getting to me."

"Do you want something for it?"

She was too embarrassed to ask for pain relief. "It's only thorn pricks."

"Fine. If that's the way you want it. But I'm going to have to go in and get them."

"Go in?" Mel raised herself up onto her elbows until she realized that she had no bra on. She quickly dropped to the examination table. "Where?"

"I've got to fish out the lone brave soul swimming energetically up your ass."

Oh God. She couldn't be more embarrassed.

"So drop your panties!" Alex said almost too gleefully.

Strike that. Yes, she could be.

"Do you need a hand?"

"I could use knockout drops and a blindfold."

"The offer still stands."

Mel sighed. Things weren't getting any better. "Let's get this over with. Go ahead." She tried to think of something positive as she felt Alex's hands rest on her hips. The slip of material went south and she couldn't help muttering "Oh Lord!" as her panties slipped off her feet.

"Holy cow!" Alex said.

"Wha— what's wrong?" Mel looked in panic over her shoulder.

"Absolutely nothing. What a magnificent ass!"

"Shoot me now," she whispered. She felt Alex's fingers pry apart her cheeks.

"Hmmm. Let me get things ready."

"Hmmm? What does that mean?"

"It means, my dear doctor, that unless you relax those cheeks of yours this is going to be tricky."

"How bad is it?" Mel glanced at her ass and then at Alex with concern.

"It's going to hurt, probably a lot."

Mel dropped her head on her forearms and instantly regretted it. "Oww." She heard the clatter of metal instruments as Alex prepared to remove the remaining thorns.

"Let me see your arm."

Before she could think, Mel obliged. She felt the prick of a needle. "Hey! What's that for?"

"I'd like some peace and quiet while I work. Besides, it'll help you sleep through the night."

It was too late to complain. The drug was already working its way through her body and the last thing she remembered was rubber-gloved fingers prising her butt cheeks apart.

Chapter Sixteen

Round Two

Mel snuggled into the blanket covering her. Its softness caressed her skin and its fresh, clean smell held a hint of hospital antiseptic. Slowly she moved about, testing her abused body. The blanket suddenly lost its softness as it scratched against her back and legs. It was only then she realized that she was on the sofa in the rec room. How did she get here? She lifted away the blanket and muttered, "Shit!"

There was a faint stirring near her and she looked to see Alex messily draped over a chair, his head drooped in uneasy sleep.

Mel looked again. She was naked. Alex had had his hands all over her and she was naked. She was going to fix that problem right now.

Unsteadily she pushed herself into an upright position. She was barely able to keep a yelp inside her as her ass hit the sofa. Mel blew out her breath forcefully and waited for the sharp pain to subside to a heavy ache. When she tried to stand she lost her balance and fell back on her ass, drawing out the yell she had tried so hard to suppress.

Alex jumped with a start, his legs flailing wildly as he tried to wake up. "Wha— Who? I didn't fall asleep, Ma, I was studying—"

Mel wanted to laugh but her body wanted to cry. What had started out as being a Good Samaritan act for a patient had turned out to be a complete mess. Quickly, she pulled the blanket around herself and slumped back on the sofa to transfer the weight to her side.

"Good morning," Alex said cheerfully.

"Good for some," Mel murmured.

"And how are you feeling?"

"Jim dandy," Mel said sarcastically. "What did you expect me to say?" Mel closed her mouth and took a deep breath. "Sorry. It's driving me crazy." She looked him in the eye. "Thanks for coming to my rescue."

"No problem. Free of charge."

"What? No favor?"

Alex grinned and held up his mobile. He jiggled it and wiggled his eyebrows.

"You didn't! Tell me you didn't!" Mel could feel the tears well up.

"Awww, come on Mel. You know me better than that. Hippocratic Oath and all that."

"I'm not in the mood for jokes, I'm afraid."

"Your clothes are a bit useless however, so you can either wear a lab coat home or put them on and make the best of it." Alex brought the clothes and Mel inspected the damage. Most of it had been shredded. Her panties were barely functional. Mel slid her hands through her hair.

She looked at the clock on the wall. Eight a.m. "Come on then. Let's get going." Mel would have quite happily stayed put but she had things to do and a car to rescue.

"Need a hand?" Alex said cheerily.

Mel gave him a stare and struggled on. "Do you mind?"

"Sure." He reached out to grab her hand.

"No. I mean leave. Now. I'm not getting dressed in front of you."

"Spoil sport."

"How about you fetch your car and I'll meet you out front?"

"If that's the way you want it." He didn't wait for her reply.

"Yeah," she sighed, "that's the way I want it." Mel inspected her clothes. "I really liked that shirt." There were more holes in the cloth than in a sieve. She took the dressing slow and steady and had to stop a couple of times to pull the cloth away when it caught on her broken skin. Finally she was dressed and gave the office one last glance before she walked carefully out the door and down the stairs.

Alex had parked outside, the engine of his car turned off. "What took you so long?"

Mel climbed in slowly and waited for the blinding stars behind her eyelids to subside. She gave him a venomous stare. "We better go by my home first so I can change."

"I'd like to be finished by eleven. I'm taking Cheryl out for lunch."

Mel felt chagrined. "I'm sorry. I've taken you away from enjoying your weekend."

"Don't worry about it." He glanced at her with a smile. "Last night made that all worthwhile."

Twenty minutes later Alex drew up to the curb smoothly and chuckled as Mel struggled out of the seat. "Give me five minutes." She was about to leave when she turned around. "Make that ten."

Fifteen minutes later she emerged from her apartment, a little more chipper than when she went in.

"You look better."

"Took a Tylenol®. Let's go get my car."

On the way, Mel finally told Alex the full story. "So when we get there I want you to run interference for me."

"I suppose I could do that. Why?"

"How can I snoop if Sandra is following me around?"

"What sort of interference are we talking about?"

"I don't know. Lock yourself in the bathroom. Spill something. Knock over a vase. Use your imagination." Mel shifted and winced. "How did the surgery go last night?"

"I had to dig out a handful of them. The one in your butt crack was a tough one."

"Hmm. No wonder it feels sore."

"Had to put a stitch in."

Mel's eyebrows rose.

"I gave you the sedative so you'd unclench your butt cheeks." Alex glanced sideways. "You could bounce a walnut off those babies."

Mel could feel the flush creep up her body.

"Your injuries are nothing serious, however you're a walking advertisement for iodine."

"Yeah, I can smell it."

"Can't be too careful."

Mel looked out the window. "No, you can't."

Twenty-five minutes later Alex's car sat outside Doris's house. "She's not here."

"Yeah, I can see that."

"You sound almost disappointed."

"Do I?" Mel wasn't sure what she felt. She had braced herself for a confrontation and now it wasn't going to happen—at least, not this morning. "Come on. Let's get this over with."

She gingerly exited the car and walked up the path to the front door.

"What if they come back?"

"Doris doesn't know they're here. We'll just tell the truth."

"That you're spying on them?"

Mel's lips pursed. "We didn't know anyone was here."

"But we know—"

"Sometimes I wonder how you managed to get your Ph.D."

"Brains, and a lot of sleepless nights."

"Uh huh." Mel didn't believe that for one minute. She slipped the key in the lock and opened the door. There was a faint smell of cooked food. Was there anyone home? Just because the car wasn't in the driveway didn't mean that the house was empty. "Hello?" she said tentatively, holding her breath in anticipation of an answer. This time the silence was reassuring. "You watch the door."

Alex stood in the hallway and kept his mouth shut while Mel read Doris's note. Quickly she collected the items on Doris's list and stacked them in the hallway. She searched for the final item, Doris's papers, bills and will, and found them haphazardly shoved in the concertina file they were stored in. Had someone gone through them or had Doris neglected to tidy up the file? Mel took a photo of the mess with her camera. She stopped at the dining room table and shuffled the papers into some semblance of order.

There was a small pile of envelopes nearby and she scanned them. Bills probably, but Mel grabbed them all the same. However, she knew that by taking them Sandra would know someone had been in the house.

Mel was torn between taking them and leaving them. Did she want to tip her hand this early? It was then that Mel hesitated. Why was she so worried about what Sandra did? It wasn't her home and Doris wasn't family. However, she did feel some remorse that she was the one who talked Doris into going to Shady Oakes. Doris was a sweet woman and if she didn't stand up for her, who would?

She looked at the envelopes again, noting the name and address of each sender. There were a couple of bills and what looked like a letter or two from friends. Conspicuously missing was anything from the bank, which set off an internal alarm. Mel put the letters down as she found them and decided that Sandra, when she deigned it necessary, would visit her mother. She again took a photo as a record.

Mel quickly roamed around the house to take more photos with her cell. She stopped at the bookshelf and removed half a dozen books to add to the pile of goods going back to Doris.

"Come on," she told Alex, "let's get out of this place."

It took four trips to get all the stuff packed in Mel's car. Alex trotted back and locked up, leaving Mel to lean against the hood of her car and watch the street.

When Alex returned he glanced at his watch. "I should make it."

"Thanks for everything."

"Go home and get some rest. If you can't make it in tomorrow, let me know."

"I should be all right. I only have a couple of patients in the morning, however my afternoon is full."

Alex climbed into his car. "Take it easy," he said as he closed the door.

Mel raised her hand as he sped off. She casually strolled to the driver's side door and looked pensively at the seat. "Oh, boy." Slowly she lowered herself into the car and shifted around gently. "Ow, ow, ow!" she whispered.

When she felt settled enough to drive, she glanced back in her rear view mirror. Her gaze shifted to the garden as she saw the rose bushes lined up in a row except, of course, for the one in the middle that she took out the night before. The side fence hid that from view so she couldn't tell whether she had critically wounded it or killed it outright.

As she contemplated that thought a car pulled up in the driveway of Doris's house. Mel didn't need to look to know it was Sandra and her family. This time her husband was also present. They each grabbed something out of the trunk and went into the house.

"Don't get too comfortable," Mel muttered as she started the engine and pulled out from the curb.

Chapter Seventeen

A Deceit Revealed

"Thank you soooo much!" Doris watched Mel and Caitlin bring her things in from Mel's car.

"What's this for?" Caitlin waved the walker she was carrying. "You don't look like you need it."

"I thought maybe Phyllis could use it."

"As if," Phyllis mumbled.

"You know very well that you can walk. You just choose not to."

"It hurts to walk."

"If you got more exercise—"

"All right, you two. We'll discuss this later." Caitlin put the walker down and went out to Mel's car. "Much more?"

"That's about it."

Caitlin brushed by Mel and saw the wince on her face. "What's wrong?"

"What do you mean?"

"You're hurt."

"It's nothing." Caitlin reached for Mel's arm and she shifted. "We're nearly finished here."

"Not until you tell me what's wrong."

"It's just an accident. I'm fine."

She faced Mel and crossed her arms. Mel ignored her and took out the final load of Doris's belongings, slipping silently past Caitlin and into the house. She deposited the box on the floor and directed her question to Doris. "Can we talk?"

"Do you want me to leave?"

"Since you seem to have a stake in this, it's okay with me. What about you, Doris?"

Doris eyed Phyllis. "I suppose so. What's wrong?"

"Sit down." Mel carefully took a seat. She wasn't aware that she was being watched but Caitlin gave her a stern look when she finally turned her attention to the women seated at the table. Mel shrugged her shoulders and held out her hands, as if to say "What?"

"Is Sandra having renovations done to her house?"

"Not that I'm aware of. Why?"

Mel's brow creased. "Did you say it was okay to let Sandra stay in your house?"

"What is going on?" Doris's voice wavered.

"I'm not sure. I went to pick up your things last night and Sandra's car was in the driveway." Mel casually glanced at each face in turn. "Your grandson came out and removed what looked like toys from the car and went back in the house."

"It doesn't worry me if they felt the need to use the house. It's just standing there empty."

"That's not the point," Phyllis said. "She should have asked first."

"Then what happened?" Caitlin asked.

"I came back the next morning and there was no car. I popped in and got your things and left."

"Maybe it was only one night. Problem solved." Doris seemed content with her conclusion.

"As I was leaving this morning they returned. I didn't stick around to see what was going on."

"Maybe they were cleaning the house in preparation to rent it out." Doris offered.

"Maybe," Mel said carefully. "It didn't look like it to me when I was inside. It just looked lived in." Mel removed her cell from her pocket. "I took some photos while I was there. Does anything look out of place?"

"What are you saying?" Doris looked at Mel, Phyllis and Caitlin. "That I can't trust my own daughter?"

Mel bit her tongue to stop her opinion from coming out. "Please, just take a look at the photos to satisfy my own curiosity." She handed the phone to Doris and waited for her answer. "Just push that button to flick to the next photo." Her finger hovered above her cell for a moment. She watched Doris's expression carefully. "So?"

"Hmmm." Doris flipped through the shots, her brow furrowed.

"Something interesting?"

"It doesn't matter. She knows she's welcome."

Doris's expression changed.

"What?" Mel leaned to see what had Doris concerned. It was the snap of the file with the papers. "That was how I found it. I'm assuming by the look on your face that it's not how you left it."

Doris handed back the phone. "Your point?"

"Doris." Mel reached her hand across the table. "I don't want to see you get hurt."

Doris stood up. "I'm going to my room."

"Did Sandra ever give you a reason why she didn't want you to move here, or why she changed her mind?"

Doris stopped. "No." She proceeded down the hallway.

"Just what is going on here?" Caitlin asked. "What are you implying?"

"I'm not implying anything. I'm saying that I think Sandra is trying to hoodwink her mother. I just don't know how or why."

"And why are you all so bent out of shape about it? She's not your mother."

"No, but I'm the one who pushed her into this."

"What do you want me to do?" Phyllis asked quietly.

"Make sure she's all right." Mel watched Phyllis roll away. "Still no wheelchair?"

"The insurance company called on Friday. They'll deliver the new one on Tuesday."

"About time. They are speed demons when it comes to collecting premiums but if they have to pay out..."

"I have to admit I was beginning to wonder when it would arrive."

"It's not here yet." Mel grinned.

Caitlin growled at her. "You are a troublemaker."

"Sure am."

"Now that we're alone, what happened to you?"

Mel sighed. "I fell into a rose bush, okay?"

Caitlin's lips curled into a smirk. "Ow?"

"Don't remind me. I had Alex pulling thorns out of my ass all night."

Caitlin's lips spread wider into a grin.

"I shouldn't have said that."

"Are you okay?"

"Why do you think I'm still standing?"

"Want a coffee?"

"Don't mind if I do. I haven't had anything since… since… last night, in fact."

Mel followed Caitlin into the kitchen. She was about to sit when Caitlin held up her finger and disappeared into the dining room. She returned with a cushion and placed it on the seat. A snide comment wanted to pass Mel's lips but she gave up, content to sit down slowly and breathe deep as the softness cushioned the pain. "Stop sniggering."

"I'm doing no such thing."

"I can feel it. Stop it." Mel growled.

Caitlin placed the mug in front of her and collected the cookie barrel. "You're grouchy. Eat something."

Mel chuckled.

"What?" Caitlin sat down with her coffee.

"We haven't even gone out on a date and you're already bossing me around."

Caitlin ducked her head.

"Hey, I'm sorry. That was uncalled for. I didn't mean to imply anything."

"No?"

To Mel, Caitlin sounded almost disappointed. "Do you want me to imply something?"

"What are we going to do about Doris?"

Mel accepted the change in topic. "I really don't know what to do. I've overstepped my bounds already."

"If it were you—"

"If it were me I'd get my mail re-directed for one thing. I don't know how long those letters had been sitting on the table. Can you take her to her bank tomorrow? That'd be a good place to start."

"And if something is hinky?"

"And if it is indeed 'hinky', as you call it, then I'd probably encourage her to drop Sandra's authority to access her account."

"Do you think it's that bad?"

"Better to be prepared for the worst."

†

Doris sat on the edge of her bed. She looked up at the sound of approaching squeaky wheels "What do you want?"

"Hey!" Phyllis grumbled. "What did I do?"

"You pushed me into this."

"Don't blame me for what you find. I'm your friend, remember?

"How could I forget?"

"I don't need sarcasm from you. If you don't want me here I can fix that." Phyllis moved her wheelchair backwards.

"Hold it." Doris sighed and looked Phyllis in the eye. "I'm sorry. I could use a friend right now."

"So you think something's wrong." It wasn't a question.

"Maybe. I don't know." Doris put her hands on her knees and squeezed. "What should I do?"

"What do you want to do?"

"I don't know. That's why I'm asking you."

"Can I ask you something? I want you to promise me not to get snippy."

"I'm worried already."

Phyllis hesitated. "What was your husband like?"

"I don't need to get snippy about that."

"I mean, did he make all the decisions and you just accepted it or did you make the decisions together?"

Doris knew what Phyllis was asking. "Are you asking was I a wimp?"

Phyllis smiled gently. "I wouldn't have put it like that, but yeah, I suppose that's what I mean."

Doris considered the question for a moment. "I suppose I was. He thought I had my hands full with the house and raising a child. It's not something that we had ever discussed. It was just the way it was."

"And Sandra? How did she treat you?"

"You mean, like father like daughter?"

"Yeah." Phyllis inched her wheelchair closer. "From what I've seen of her, she seems pretty intent on running your life."

"I don't mind."

"There you go again. When you're here, you're great! Ah, I mean you have no problem in expressing yourself. As soon as she shows up you crawl back into your shell. Grow a backbone, girl!"

"I'm sorry. It's hard to change the habit of a lifetime."

"Don't be sorry. She has no right to run your life."

"What about when I can no longer look after myself? She's the one who has the control as to where I live."

Doris watched Phyllis's mouth open and close. "We'll look after you. You're part of our family now."

"And if that changes, what happens?"

"What makes you think it will change? We look after our own."

"And if Caitlin moves on? Or the house burns down? What do we do then?"

"Caitlin is well aware of what she started. She won't abandon us, at least not until she finds someone to take her place. I've known her long enough to know she isn't that sort of a woman. As for everything else, let's not worry about things that might not happen."

"But—"

"It's too beautiful a day to worry about such things. How about we go for a walk, and I'll even use that walker of yours."

"How can I refuse an offer like that?" Doris stood and moved behind Phyllis's wheelchair. She pushed it back to the living room and fetched the walker from the corner. Phyllis eyed the

125

contraption warily. "We'll start off slow and only walk a few hundred feet," Doris said.

"Okay."

"Second thoughts?"

"Hey, it got you out of your room."

"Pleased with yourself?"

"Yep." Phyllis beamed at Doris, who couldn't resist returning the smile. "Come on. Let's go before I change my mind."

"Where are you two going?" Caitlin asked from the kitchen doorway.

"I'm just going for a short walk with my friend here." Phyllis smiled at Caitlin and winked. She struggled to stand and allowed Doris to move the walker in front of her. It moved easily and she found the device quite simple to use. "We should be only a few minutes."

"Be careful."

"Oh, and by the way, Doris wants to go to the bank tomorrow."

"I do?"

"Yep," Phyllis replied, "Because you want to get your mail re-directed and to check on your bank balance."

"I do?"

"Yes, you do." Phyllis pushed the walker out the door and onto the driveway. "Now let's roll."

Doris shrugged and followed Phyllis out the door.

Mel stepped up beside Caitlin. "Well, that solves the problem of getting her to the bank."

Caitlin turned to go back in the kitchen. "I'll have to add 'mind reader' to the list of Phyllis's accomplishments."

✝

Phyllis shuffled along. While the pain in her hip was still there it was tempered by the weight she could put on the walker.

"You surprised me," Doris said.

"About what?" Phyllis tried to keep her attention on the walker in case it got away from her.

"I didn't think you would take to that thing."

"I painted myself into a corner. It was either use it or lose it."

"I wouldn't do that to you."

Phyllis looked up quickly from the ground. "Probably not, but what would my word be worth if I had backed out?"

They took another step down the sidewalk, then another.

"I think I'm getting the hang of this." However the focus it took to keep the walker upright and the energy to push it along was telling on her.

"It's hard at first, but it becomes easier as time goes on."

"Is that from personal experience?"

"I broke my ankle about ten years ago. The physio put me onto it. Like you, I was rather fond of my wheelchair, but it was cumbersome."

"And your husband didn't like it?" Phyllis said lightly.

"Hmm," Doris hummed. She ducked her head and looked at the garden they were passing.

"Sorry."

"Are you all right? Do you want to continue?"

"We can go a little further if you want." Phyllis didn't want the walk to end, despite what her hip was trying to tell her. "We'll be going to the library on Thursday. Caitlin will see to getting you signed up."

"Find anything interesting while you were there?"

"Maybe. I haven't decided yet. They didn't have any lesbian literature though."

"And that's important to you?"

"Not really, but the fact that they didn't have it made me mad."

Doris stopped. "Let me get this straight. The library didn't have any lesbian books and you're mad, despite the fact that you have no interest in reading them or that you won't read any of them even if there were any."

Phyllis thought for a minute. "That's about it in a nutshell. They should have them irrespective of whether I would read them or not."

127

Doris's mouth flapped about silently. "I don't get it," she said finally.

"You're not supposed to. While it is a moot point I wanted to point it out… noisily."

"Did you complain?"

"No." Phyllis observed Doris's pursed lips. "The kid who was stacking the books gave me a disgruntled look. What could I say?"

"And you talk about me being a wimp…" Doris muttered under her breath.

"I heard that! I was not a wimp. I was… was…," Phyllis thought quickly, "waiting for an opportunity to press my case."

"Uh huh." Doris clicked her tongue. "Wimp."

Doris smiled at her and Phyllis felt a flutter in her chest. She only hoped it wasn't a heart attack. "Takes one to know one." Phyllis smiled sweetly back.

"What's that smile for?"

"Nothing." No, nothing at all.

Chapter Eighteen

Fallen Hero

"So, Mrs. Hansen. What can we do for you today?"

The bank worker had a fake smile plastered on and his upbeat, chirpy demeanor made Caitlin want to throw up. It was the same sickening smile she got when her banker told her she was overdrawn.

"I'd like to have my statements delivered to a different address."

"That isn't a problem." He reached into the second drawer of the filing cabinet behind him and pulled out a form. "Just fill this out and we'll make the change for you immediately."

"Can you tell me my balance?"

"Your account number?"

"I don't have it with me. Can't you look it up?"

The smile dropped a little bit when he sighed deeply. Customer service had slipped a notch. "Let's seeee." The word slurred for a moment or two as he typed in her name on the computer. "Ahh. It's one hundred and twenty three thousand seven hundred and sixty-two dollars, and thirteen cents."

Doris looked up from the form she was filling in.

"Something wrong?" Caitlin asked. She inched forward toward the table.

"There was a large sum withdrawn about four weeks ago. It says here that you were contacted, but your daughter said you were unavailable. She confirmed the amount."

Caitlin watched Doris's brow crease. "Does it say who the amount was made out to?"

The clerk looked to Doris for confirmation. "Yes... please," she said reluctantly. It was almost as if Doris didn't want to know.

He viewed the screen. "Two hundred and fifty thousand dollars was transferred to your daughter's bank account."

"Two hun—?" Caitlin was flabbergasted. She'd consider herself lucky if she had two thousand in her bank account.

"We thought you were aware of this transaction." He looked nervously at Doris.

"Yes, I knew about it, now that you mention it. I'd forgotten. It's my age, you know."

"Surely." He breathed a sigh of relief. Caitlin knew it was more relief for his employment rather than Doris losing her money.

"I can't find my statements for the last six months. Could you please—?"

"One moment," he said before she even had a chance to finish her sentence. He jumped up out of his seat and disappeared out the door.

"Doris."

"Don't! Please don't." Doris slumped back in her chair. Caitlin could see her confidence was shattered. She had been right, but at what price?

"Don't you think it would be a good idea to suspend Sandra's access to your account, at least until you get this sorted out?"

"Are you saying I shouldn't trust my daughter?" Doris said angrily.

"Has she given you any reason to?" Caitlin replied. "Look, it doesn't have to be a permanent thing. Just until you've had a chance to talk to her."

"Since the money is already gone it seems rather pointless, don't you think?"

"I suppose it is, but it would at least show her she can't take advantage of you like that."

Doris said nothing before she turned her attention back to the paper on the table.

Caitlin sat back worried. She watched Doris fill out the form and wondered what was in store for her. Phyllis seemed to have a rapport with her. Could she help Doris to cope with the shock?

Caitlin sat silently until the clerk returned. "There you go, Mrs. Hansen."

Doris handed him the finished form and he perused it. "This shouldn't be a problem. If there's anything else…"

"Please suspend my daughter's access to my account."

The bank assistant's eyebrows rose. "Permanently?"

"Until I tell you otherwise."

"Is there a problem I should know about?" He looked from Doris to Caitlin, and back again.

"I think there has been a misunderstanding between us," Doris said.

"Is it something to do with the withdrawal?" He fiddled with his pen, obviously anxious he had done something wrong.

"She's not pointing a finger at the bank," Caitlin interrupted. "It's something that needs to be sorted out, that's all."

"Fine, I will attend to that for you, Mrs. Hansen."

"One final thing," Doris said quietly, "I want to arrange a regular withdrawal on the fifteenth of every month. Caitlin will give you the details of the amount and the bank account."

The clerk looked at Caitlin expectantly, handing her a writing pad and a pen. Doris had come to the bank with a list of things to do. She, herself, had forgotten all about it, but Doris had the state of mind to remember it. It was all too much. Caitlin shook her head and began to write.

†

"Thought I might find you here." Phyllis walked slowly from the back door to the seat by the wall.

"Where's your wheelchair?"

"I didn't think I'd need it."

She sat down carefully and sighed when the weight came off her feet. She looked at Doris in sympathy.

"Don't say it!" Doris snapped.

"I wasn't going to say anything." Phyllis said no more, much to Doris's surprise.

They both gazed out at the backyard, observing a couple of blue jays chasing one another around the garden.

"Ahh, there you are."

Both women turned to look at the owner of the voice stepping out onto the porch. Sophie smiled back. "Smooth."

Phyllis scowled at her.

"What is she talking about?"

"Nothing," Phyllis growled.

"Don't mind me."

"I won't. Now, get lost."

Sophie held up her hands. "Sorr-ee for butting in. You and your honey go back to whatever you were doing."

"Honey? Phyllis, what does she mean?"

"Sophie! Will you shut up!"

Sophie backed away and left Phyllis to her dilemma. She felt Doris shift back an inch or two. "Just ignore her."

Phyllis could see that the moment was lost, interrupted by a woman whose sex drive had ploughed into her, only to leave before seeing the carnage left behind. "Excuse me for a moment." Phyllis stood and stretched her aging body. The creak coming from her hip didn't worry her, but the snap did. Maybe it was time to see the doc. She shuffled back into the house to have a word with Sophie.

✝

"Sophie, sometimes you can be such a bitch!" Phyllis growled as she stood in the doorway to Sophie's room.

"What's the matter?"

"You said something so monumentally stupid I can't believe it came out of your mouth. No, I take that back. I can, and it did."

"Come on now, Phyll. I was only saying what we all thought."

"I was not, I repeat NOT, trying to hit on Doris."

"Deny it all you want—"

"Shut up!" Phyllis yelled. "She got some bad news and I was comforting her."

"Comfort. Yeah, I've heard it called that—"

Phyllis walked forward. "I'm going to pound you into next week!"

132

"What's going on?" Isabel appeared at the door.

Phyllis turned to stare at her new opponent. "Don't you start!" She swivelled back to face Sophie. "It's about time you grow up, Soph. We've put up with your lesbian bullshit because you were new to the game and caught up in your own wishful thinking. Your unnatural fascination with the female anatomy has overstepped the mark and it's now time to get a life."

"I was just trying to—"

"Well, it ain't working. It's juvenile and it's heading toward being weird. It certainly won't get you a woman."

"Then, what do I do?" Sophie asked quietly.

"Why is it so important?" Isabel asked.

"Because I don't want to die without knowing what it's like."

Phyllis looked at Isabel for some support. "Did your doctor ever talk to you about menopause?"

"Sure. Why?"

"You *do* know that your sex drive is supposed to slow down, not go into overdrive. Right?"

"Yeah. So?"

"You are acting like a lovesick teenager. Cut it out!"

"What she's trying to say, without much success, is that now that you are heading into your twilight years the likelihood of you getting laid is bordering on zero."

"Nice one, Izzy," Phyllis muttered.

"What? I'm not saying anything that isn't true."

"And tact to you is a bar of soap."

"Well, hello pot!"

"Both of you, stop it!" Sophie yelled. Her eyes closed. "So that's it, huh?"

"Look, we're not saying it isn't impossible, we're just saying that it's unlikely. You could be one of the lucky ones."

"Lucky? Sounds more like lucked out." Sophie studied Phyllis as she took a seat. "At least you had a chance when you were younger."

"It's not a lucky dip, Soph. You made your choice to get married. I didn't even know you then."

"No, you were out making history. It sounded pretty exciting to me."

"Yeah, well, it wasn't all heroics back then."

"What happened?" Isabel asked.

Phyllis could feel Isabel's eyes on her, as if she could read the deceit there. "I didn't make any history."

"Huh," Sophie mumbled. "That's more than you've ever said about the matter before."

Doris's words swirled around in her head. Had she made more of the incident all these years than was really necessary? She hadn't thought so. She truly felt that she was a fraud. But Doris didn't see it that way. Could she have been wrong? Phyllis bit the bullet. "I wasn't involved in the riot."

"You weren't there?"

Phyllis heard the sadness in Sophie's voice.

"I was there all right. When things started to get ugly, I ran." She closed her eyes so she didn't have to see the disappointment in Sophie's eyes.

"Why?"

"That's a question I've asked myself many times. The only reason I could come up with was that I didn't want to end up a vegetable."

"What are you talking about?"

"Did you think we'd get a slap on the wrist for what happened? Being arrested for being gay was one thing, being openly hostile about it is a completely different thing. I'd already been in jail once, just because I dressed differently. I swore I wouldn't go back."

"Why didn't you say this in the first place?"

"Because, Izzy, I was embarrassed. I betrayed my fellow brothers and sisters. I abandoned them to their fate."

"You were one person, Phyll."

"And if everyone thought like that, no one would have stood up to them. Every single one counts." There was silence. "You've got nothing to say?" Phyllis asked Sophie.

"Isabel is right. You were one person. One lonely, homeless person."

"I didn't say I was homeless."

"But you did say you had a falling out with your family. Unless you had a great paying job, you would have been living hard."

"I have the philosophy that what we do in the past affects how we shape our future," Isabel declared.

"Really? You're a therapist now?"

Isabel smiled. "I'm a professor. It covers a lot of subjects."

"Stop beating yourself up about this," Sophie answered. "It was a long time ago."

Phyllis didn't know what to make of it all. She was terrified that if Sophie found out what had happened she'd lose that look of idolization. She liked being a hero in her eyes... in everyone's eyes. Stonewall was not one of her finest moments.

"You said you got yourself a job?" Isabel asked.

Phyllis looked down at her hands. A lot of water had passed under that particular bridge. "A few of us had broken into a nearby church and slept in the basement when it got cold, and God, it got cold. They must have figured it out because a week or so later blankets appeared, then an old mattress or two and some food. One night the priest was there waiting for us. We got talking and he worked hard to get us jobs. Some of them were pretty nasty, but one job led to another, slightly better one until I could look after myself."

"See?" Sophie said. "Some good came out of it after all."

"You really don't care, do you?" Phyllis was surprised.

"I like *you*, Phyll, not what you did."

"But you always made a fuss about Stonewall."

"It was the only thing I knew about you. What else could I say?"

"Huh," Phyllis muttered. "All this time..."

"What brought this up? I mean, why are you telling us this now?"

"I was going to talk to Doris about facing her demons with her daughter. I suppose I thought I should practice what I preached."

She looked at Sophie sheepishly. "Besides, I was so mad at you I thought if I told you the truth I'd piss you off."

Sophie laughed. "Now I've pissed you off more for taking the news well." Her smile dropped. "What do I do?"

"About what?"

"My lesbian dilemma. Don't you listen?"

"I did, but that was ages ago." She saw Sophie's façade drop. "You need to get out more. Maybe join a group."

"I thought I already had."

"We know better, so you have no hope here. Try an art class. From what I saw of your drawings they weren't bad. Or you could try a recreational group."

"But won't that cost money?"

"It won't cost you money to ask. If it does, talk to Caitlin to see if it can be worked into the budget."

"What was the problem that had gotten you all riled up?" Isabel asked.

"Caitlin told me Doris just found out Sandra's been dipping her hand in the till."

"Damn," Sophie muttered.

"Too right," Isabel added.

"So what do we do?"

"I was told to butt out. It's none of our business," Phyllis declared.

"Now the daughter has moved into mom's home. What's going on? If we won't help her, who will?" Sophie looked from Phyllis to Isabel.

"I can't do anything. I promised Caitlin."

"But we didn't."

"I can't be a part of this. I'm leaving. And *you*," Phyllis pointed at Sophie, "no more comments about me and Doris. Got it?"

"Got it." Sophie sat there suitably humbled.

Phyllis shuffled out of the room and headed toward the back door.

Sophie looked at Isabel. "Izzy, I've got a job for you."

Chapter Nineteen

An Unexpected Question

"I heard shouting. Is everything all right?"

"Sorry about that. I had to see an idiot about a moronic statement. All sorted." Phyllis sat down with a grunt. "I've been on my feet too long."

"Do you need your wheelchair?"

"Not at the moment. I'm happy to sit here with you." Phyllis felt the slight withdrawal. "Nothing's going to happen. Sophie was spewing garbage." She looked at Doris. "I just want to be your friend, nothing more."

"Do you think I'm pretty?"

Phyllis's jaw dropped. "Where did that come from?"

"I don't know. I suppose you trying to convince me that you're not attracted to me. I'm not ugly, am I?"

"Whatever gave you that idea? I didn't say that."

"So I *am* attractive?"

"I didn't say that either. There is no answer to that question that won't get me into trouble." Phyllis could feel her defences rising.

"Of course there is. You could say 'yes'."

"And if I say 'yes' you'll be thinking I'm trying to put the moves on you."

"Put the moves?"

Phyllis cleared her throat. "Trying to seduce you," she mumbled.

"Would you?"

Phyllis nibbled her lower lip. "Another loaded question." She inched her way along the seat, putting distance between herself and Doris. "How did we get onto this subject?"

137

"You were trying to comfort me and it got me wondering."

"What was your husband's name?"

"Husband?"

"The one you married all those years ago. Sandra's dad."

"Norman. Why do you want to know that?"

"Just reminding you which side of the fence you are on."

"I don't get it. I thought you'd be jumping at the chance to convert me."

"No, you don't get it. It's not some sort of religious sect. This is about who we really are inside, not who we worship. We've all had this epiphany in our lives, and it's not one that can be decided by strong-arm tactics."

"What's it like?"

"It's liberating; to finally be what you'd always known in your heart. In my instance, it didn't come without pain and shame."

"No, I meant to be with a wo… woman." Doris blushed.

Phyllis chuckled and looked at the beans on the vines in the garden. "Not having been with a man leaves me at a disadvantage, but being with a woman can be an intense experience. In the early days those moments were fleeting. You always had one eye looking over your shoulder in case someone spotted you or, worse, it was the cops. Things are better now, but not perfect. At least you don't worry about ending up in some psych ward."

"That sounds barbaric."

"Back in the Sixties, it was. So was racial segregation in the Fifties. This country was run by bigoted, narrow-minded fools."

"And now?"

"Still run by bigoted, narrow-minded fools, but with more people watching it's hard for them get away with everything."

"So, how do you… you know."

Phyllis knew what she meant. "You know? I know what?" she teased.

Doris's blush darkened. "How do you…," Doris cleared her throat. "Make love?"

"Hardly ever these days."

"Oh, come on. I didn't say when, I said how."

Phyllis could see Doris was losing her patience. "I suppose the big thing, or the little thing in this case, is the lack of certain things. Appendages. Then, as I said, it's more emotionally intense and lasts a heck of a lot longer. I've been told it's different from a guy. A good different."

Doris stared out over the back yard, apparently absorbing the information. "Huh."

"Any other embarrassing questions?"

Doris smiled shyly at her. "That's all for now."

"Feeling better?"

"Thanks. The news shook me up a little."

"I'd probably be taking Sandra into some quiet corner to have a talk with her, but I'm not you. Have you decided what you're going to do?"

"Not yet. I'm still getting over the shock of it."

"Give yourself a few days to settle down before you make any decision."

"Sage advice."

"One learned from constantly putting my foot in my mouth. Many times I wished I'd thought first before acting."

†

Mel took a breather from her caseload. It had been a busy morning, in a long line of busy days. Her mind slipped to Caitlin and the home and wondered what they were up to. It had been quiet. Too quiet.

A knock on the door drew her attention. "Come in."

Caroline entered with mug in hand. "I thought you could use this." She put it down on Mel's desk.

"I really should cut down on this stuff."

"You say that all the time and I've yet to see you take any notice."

"You're not helping."

"If I hadn't brought the coffee in, would you have got one yourself?"

"That's not the point."

"That is precisely my point, Doctor. All I'm doing is cutting down on the shoe leather. To say 'no' is your department."

She was right and Mel knew that. "When the stress in my life ends then I can think about giving up coffee."

"What stress? You know very well that I run this office." Caroline winked at her. "What's the problem?"

Mel looked up at her receptionist leaning on the patient's chair. Talking to Alex would only get smart remarks. "What about your Hippocratic Oath?"

Caroline took her finger and crossed her heart. "Okay, that's done. Now, what is your problem?"

"It's a certain retirement home owner."

"Caitlin, you mean."

"Ho… how did you know about her?" There could be only one source. "I'll kill him!"

"Now, now. Hold your horses." Caroline moved from behind the chair to sit on it. "He was worried about you."

"Worried? What was there to worry about?"

"We both know you work too hard. You have no love life and you run to that home at the drop of a hat. It doesn't take a genius to figure it out."

"I wish she would." Mel reached for the mug and took a sip. She let out a noisy *ahhh* as she enjoyed the liquid sliding down her throat.

"Have you told her you're interested?"

"Well, not in so many words. I've dropped the odd hint here and there."

"Maybe it's time to be a little less subtle."

"How obvious do you want me to be?"

"A kiss should do it."

"A ki— Are you nuts?"

"What is wrong with you? You like the girl. She's available and lesbian. Grab those non-existent balls of yours and make a move."

"And if she's not interested?"

"Do you think she's not?"

Mel thought about that. What contact she had with Caitlin was pleasant. While they had not discussed a date, Mel had thought that Caitlin, in her own subtle way, had sent her the right signals that she was interested. Why was she hesitating? "I don't think so. I had put it out there a while back and she changed the subject."

Caroline plucked at her lip while she thought. "Maybe she wasn't sure what you felt. After all, you are the doctor and her girls are your patients."

"May-beee." Mel's eyes went out of focus as she tried to remember her previous meetings with Caitlin. Had she ever called her Mel? She couldn't remember. She definitely remembered 'Dr. Stokes' or 'the doctor', but Mel?

"You'll probably have to be the one to make the first move."

A wide grin grew on Mel's lips. "You may be right." She looked directly into Caroline's eyes. "Thanks."

"That's what you pay me the big bucks for." She stood and made her way to the door.

"I do not."

"Then maybe you should." Caroline winked at her before leaving.

"Maybe I should," Mel whispered.

†

Tuesday came and Phyllis was on the edge of her dented wheelchair seat. The morning came and went without any sight of a delivery man.

Caitlin emerged from the kitchen to watch Phyllis sitting by the front door. "Will you stop rocking in that chair? The squeak is really annoying."

"Where is he?"

Caitlin chuckled. "You sound like a kid on Christmas morning wondering if Santa has delivered his presents." Phyllis glared at her. "Hmmm, I suppose it is just that. Coffee?"

"Is that your answer to everything? I can see the doc's point now. We are all slowly drowning in a sea of coffee."

"Tea then." Caitlin turned around and left Phyllis alone. She heard a noise and looked around to find Doris at the dining room table shaking a box. "Up for Scrabble®? Maybe we can even play it properly this time."

"Sure. What have I got to lose?" Phyllis swung her wheelchair around to face Doris.

"I haven't told you the wager yet."

"Yeah? This sounds interesting."

"If you lose you have to get out of that chair more often. You rely on it too much."

"It's painful to walk."

"And it's painful to watch, but you need your exercise. I'll walk with you."

"Let me think about it." Was the pain worth Doris's company? Phyllis wasn't sure about that one. "And if I win?"

"You get out of that chair more often."

"That's a lose-lose situation. You have to give me some incentive to play."

"Hmmm. I'll buy you a bag of cookies."

"That sort of goes against the whole exercise thing, don't you think?"

"True, but it may give you an incentive to get out of—"

"—that thing. I get the point."

"You are going to drive yourself crazy sitting around waiting for the delivery man. I'm sure Caitlin is quite capable of signing the delivery notice herself."

"You were sent here by God, weren't you? You're here to be my nemesis."

"I thought we were getting along quite well."

"That's all part of the plan. Pull me in with your sweet talk and cheerful smile. Then, when I least expect it, you pounce and the next thing I know you've hidden the wheelchair and I'm left to my own devices." Doris smiled at her. "See?"

"Do you want to play or not?"

Phyllis looked wistfully at the front door. "Sure, why not? Maybe it'll be a draw and I won't have to give up the chair. You *do* realize that I'm getting a new one. It sort of contradicts the purpose of the bet."

"Put up or shut up."

"Oooh, a serious player. I like that. Grab your tiles, Hansen."

†

The chair finally arrived close to five o'clock. Phyllis was a nervous wreck.

"About bloody time!"

"What is your problem?" Doris said as she put the game on the sideboard.

"It would be just like them not to deliver."

"What! The delivery company?"

"No, the insurance company."

"Why would they show up? They only pay for the thing, not deliver it."

"No, not show up, pay for it. It... It.... Don't confuse me. Those sleazy companies are always finding ways of not paying out."

"Did it happen to you before? It certainly sounds like you've had a bad experience."

"A long time ago, and I'm sure they haven't improved since then."

"Want to tell me about it?"

"Not really. Short version is a truck ran into the back of my bike. The insurance company tried to put the blame on me by saying I stopped suddenly. I'm not stupid! I knew the truck was behind me. Did they honestly think I'd do that, knowing very well that the thing behind me would wipe me off the road? What sort of idiot do they take me for?"

"Let me guess, this is why you sit in this wheelchair."

"Damned straight. Poor Leslie was written off. Damned I miss her."

"Your passenger?"

"My bike. They eventually paid up but it barely covered all the medical expenses. Instead of the six million dollar man, I'm the thirty-five thousand dollar and some change woman."

"Wow! That's some bill."

"They re-built me to be even slower than I was before."

"They probably did that to keep you off the road. You are a menace." Doris added a smile to ease the joke.

Phyllis glowered at first, then let the emotion slip away, replacing it with a smile. "You're probably right. I was getting too old to be living on the road. Mornings were really beginning to piss me off."

"Let's take a look at your new wheels. Is that the right word?"

"Sure is. I feel like I've been transported back to the Seventies."

The chair was sitting by the door and Phyllis approached it tentatively. Did she want a new chair? Her old one had been her constant companion for a few years now and she was loathe to give it up.

"Give it a chance. The new one may even grow on you."

Had Doris read her mind? "I hope not, otherwise I'd never stand up again." Doris's quizzical look made her add, "Grow on you. Would I transplant myself onto the chair?"

"Oh, you had me wondering. Funny," Doris said drolly. "It looks nice."

"We'll see," Phyllis looked at the plastic wrapped chair with some disdain. "We'll see."

Chapter Twenty

The Plot Thickens

"Have you found anything?" Phyllis leaned heavily on her wheelchair and watched Isabel's fingers fly over the keyboard.

"Give me a minute."

"We don't have a minute." She observed Caitlin on her way across the library. "Here she comes."

"What's so interesting that has you two hovering over a computer?" Caitlin asked.

"Nothing," they said in unison.

"Right." Phyllis could see that she didn't believe them for one minute.

"We're working on Doris's problem."

"Doris has a problem?" Phyllis pursed her lips and glared at Caitlin. "Oh, that problem. It's none of our business."

"I thought we were all in this together. Have I got it wrong?"

Caitlin sighed. "No, but Doris may not want us sticking our noses in her business."

"We won't tell her unless we find something wrong."

"Which is why I'm doing a search on Sandra's property," Isabel said.

"What's that got to do with anything?"

"Why is Sandra living in Doris's house if she has one of her own?"

"Exterminators? Renovations?"

Phyllis frowned. "Okay. They are valid points." She didn't like being wrong, and Sandra's behavior said 'wrong' in big red letters.

"Hang on." Isabel moved closer to the screen and squinted. "There's a listing here for Sandra's house."

"Listing? As in sale?"

"Listing, as in rent. She's put her own place up for rent."

"Why that…." Phyllis barely held onto the cuss words buzzing around in her mouth. This was a library after all. "I think that constitutes wrong in my book. Time to tell Doris."

†

Alice had been thinking about it for a while. Someone really needed to do a reconnaissance of the enemy. It didn't seem that anyone was volunteering for the mission, so she would go herself. Without intelligence, they could not form a battle plan.

The time was early and the weather looked like it would remain favorable. She visited the kitchen and grabbed two lots of rations and some water. She had no idea how long the journey would take but without rations or water her mission would be short-lived.

Before she had a chance to make her escape Caitlin appeared in the doorway.

"You're up early. Anything wrong?"

Alice quickly shoved the rations back in the refrigerator. "No. Just hungry. What's for breakfast?"

"The usual." Caitlin eyed her suspiciously. "What are you up to?"

"I might grab a shower, Captain. I'll be back later." Alice left quickly. She knew Caitlin's gaze followed her.

"I thought you were hungry." Caitlin's voice carried down the hallway.

"I've lost my appetite… for now," Alice grumbled. Now she had to have a shower before she could leave. Her plan to start early had been derailed by the Captain.

Twenty minutes later Alice once again stood in the kitchen. Unfortunately, this time Isabel and Doris were also up. Unless she left without provisions, she had to bide her time.

The morning drifted by and by the time she was ready to leave ten o'clock had come and gone. Swiftly, Alice grabbed her rations from the refrigerator and dashed out the front door. The other women were busy with their own projects and were oblivious to her plans. With some luck, she should be back in a matter of hours. If she was *really* lucky, no one would miss her.

†

"Stokes," Mel said absently as she sat in her office.

"Help! Alice!"

"Slow down!" Mel interrupted a frenzied Caitlin. "What's wrong?"

"Alice. She's missing."

"When?"

"I only found out now. Isabel says she hasn't seen Alice for a couple of hours."

Mel bit her lip. "Okay, you stay with the others and I'll go out and look."

"But, Alice—"

"Caitlin!" Mel yelled above Caitlin's panicked plea. "Your responsibility is to those women. They need you." Mel grabbed her coat, bag and keys and headed out the door. "I'll call you." She hung up her phone before Caitlin could say another word.

"Caroline," Mel said urgently as she passed the reception desk, "I have an emergency. See if you can re-schedule this afternoon's appointments please."

"Mr. Brown cancelled this morning!" Caroline called after her.

That meant she had one remaining appointment at the end of the day. Would she be lucky enough to get back in time? Lucky? Mel knew that word was in sparse use lately. Since meeting the girls from Shady Oakes luck, for her, had flown out the window.

She ran to her car then threw her possessions on to the front passenger seat before scrambling in behind the wheel. "How do they do it?"

It took thirty minutes to reach the retirement home before she could even begin her search. As tempted as she was to see Caitlin, she knew it would only delay her.

Mel did a U-turn outside Caitlin's house and headed down the street. For the next hour she systematically checked each and every street within a two mile radius of the house. When that failed, Mel expanded her search another mile in all directions. She was about to give up and call the police when she spotted a child sitting on a brick fence. As she got closer she could see it wasn't a child but an old woman. In fact, it was the one specific old woman she had been looking for.

Mel pulled up with a screech and jumped out of the car. Her parking was askew but she didn't care. All that mattered was that she had found Alice and Caitlin could stop worrying.

"Hey, I've got you." Alice fell into Mel's arms and held on tight. "What are you doing so far away from home?"

"I...I...g-g-got l-l-lost," Alice said amid a flurry of sobs. "I don't know where I am."

"Shhh," Mel brushed Alice's hair lightly. "It's all right. I'll take you to Caitlin, okay?"

"Okay." Alice pulled out of Mel's grasp and took a deep breath. "Thank you."

Alice's answers made Mel ask the question. "Alice? Why are you here?"

"I thought I knew. It's there in my head but I can't seem to focus on it."

Mel led her to her car and helped her into the front seat. Once she was buckled in Mel took her place behind the wheel. She took out her cell and looked at it "Damn, I left Caitlin's number at home," she muttered.

"It's 555 9098," Alice replied.

Mel looked at her astounded. She dialed the number.

"Hello?"

"Caitlin?"

"Mel? You found her?"

Mel could hear the relief in her voice. "Yes, she's fine. I'm bringing her home."

"Thank you."

"You can thank me in person." Mel hung up. It had been a harrowing couple of hours. "Okay Alice, let's go home."

✝

"Oh God, Alice, are you all right?" Caitlin rushed to the passenger door and pulled it open. "You had us all worried, young lady."

Mel hopped out of the car and went around to the other side of the car to help Alice out. "I think she's fine. She just became confused and got lost."

"Let's get you inside." Caitlin supported Alice on one side while Mel took the other. They guided her gently to her room and left Phyllis, Sophie and Isabel to fuss around her while they moved into the corridor.

"Where did you find her?" Caitlin whispered as she steered Mel toward the kitchen.

"A couple of miles away. She was sitting on a brick fence."

"Thank you for finding her."

"My...," Mel took a step toward Caitlin, moving to within inches of her, "... pleasure."

"Ahh, w-w-would you like a coffee?" Caitlin squeaked.

"Sure. After..."

"After?"

"After this." Mel leaned in and gently pressed her lips against Caitlin's. She stepped back and waited for a response.

"Why did you do that?"

"Because I've wanted to for a long, long time. I promised myself to kiss you the next time I saw you. However, if you don't want me to—" Before Mel had a chance to finish the sentence Caitlin stepped forward and returned the kiss. It was warm and chaste, but it felt oh, so nice. Mel swept up Caitlin into her arms and drew her closer to deepen the kiss.

"Ahem."

149

Both women broke away from one another and looked at the source of the sound.

"Don't mind me, but Alice is asking for you." Isabel said before she smiled.

"Who? Me or her?" Mel asked.

"Specifically Caitlin, but I suppose you'd do in a pinch." She trotted back down the corridor giggling.

"Oh boy, that's torn it."

"Torn? Where?"

"Isabel will tell everyone."

"As if it's a secret," Mel said.

"Well, I didn't know."

"Why do you think they've been inventing illnesses to get me here?"

"They have? Why those—"

"Leave them be. By your response it was what we all wanted. We were just a little slow to do anything about it."

Caitlin smacked Mel's shoulder and turned to leave.

"One more thing. It's time to think about better security for this place."

Caitlin sighed. "As much as I hate to admit it, I think you're right."

Mel allowed Caitlin to walk in first while she followed close behind. "She needs her rest." Mel looked at each woman until they moved. Finally there was only Alice, Caitlin and Mel left in the room.

"Are you all right?" Caitlin asked with concern.

"I... I don't know what happened."

"Don't you worry about that. We'll look after you." Caitlin patted Alice's clothed leg.

Mel watched the conversation with interest. With her sanity restored, Alice looked every day of her eighty years. She sat hunched and downcast in her bed, visibly shaken by her ordeal. The spark Caitlin had spoken of was missing in Alice, and Mel nearly wished for Alice to be the Resistance fighter again.

"Alice?"

The old woman cast a glance in Mel's direction.

"What does the second world war mean to you?"

"Pardon?" Alice looked confused.

"Did something happen?" Mel asked.

"Doctor—" Caitlin interrupted.

"No, let me ask this, okay? You would have been a child, am I right?" Alice nodded.

"My family was in northern France in 1943. The Nazis swept through the village we were staying in. My father was killed and my mother...," Alice hesitated, "...I never saw my mother again. I hid in the roof."

"That's enough for now."

"One more question... please. Were you part of a trapeze group?"

"How did you know?"

"Just a hunch. Now you get some rest." Mel motioned Caitlin to follow her out into the corridor. "That explains a lot."

"It sure does. How did you know she'd answer you?"

"I didn't, but it seemed an opportunity I couldn't pass up. It answers the question why she is fixated on the Resistance."

"She would have been about ten when it happened."

"It's a tough thing to happen to lose both parents that way." Mel wandered toward her bag and picked it up. "Now you know why she acts the way she does. Mind over matter, Caitlin."

"Pardon?"

"You said she was on the roof at one point. As far as her mind is concerned she's only a teenager and her body is trying to respond to that." Mel walked to the front door. "But her body may not take everything her mind wants to do."

"So what do I do?"

"Treat her as you always have, but make sure she doesn't do anything too stupid. Her bones won't mend as well as they used to." When Caitlin was close enough, Mel leaned in and placed a kiss on her cheek. "I'll call you later and check up on her. If you need me, I'm only a phone call away."

"Thanks." Caitlin smiled sweetly. "She scared the life out of me."

"You weren't the only one." Mel opened the door and stepped through. She gave Caitlin one final smile before walking to her car. Once behind the wheel, Mel took a deep breath. There were so many things running through her mind she didn't know which one to pay attention to.

†

"So," Phyllis said from the doorway, "what happened?"

"Everything is fuzzy. What date is it?"

"October twelfth, why?"

"Oct... which year?"

"2013."

"2013? I can't seem to remember anything since 2012. Was... was I in a coma or something?"

"Don't be daft, woman!" Phyllis rolled her wheelchair closer to Alice's bed. "You were in your own little dream world."

"What are you talking about?"

"Dementia. You have dementia."

"Don't be silly."

"Then don't believe me."

"Did I do something stupid?"

"Pick a date. You did lots of stupid things, but none of them life-threatening... at least, none that I know of."

"Don't be ridiculous. I'm eighty years old!" Alice said crankily.

"That's not my fault. You were kind of sweet as a Resistance fighter."

Alice shook her head. "Maybe you're the one with the dementia and you're hallucinating that I'm a resistance fighter."

"That's a possibility, but I doubt it."

Caitlin appeared at the door. "Feeling a bit better?"

"I'm not living in World War II if that's what you're saying."

"Errr... no, not really. I was wondering if you were feeling dizzy or confused." Caitlin looked from Alice to Phyllis.

"I just brought her up to date. She seems to think we're the ones who have dementia."

152

"Or maybe in her dementia she thinks we're demented, but in reality it's her dementia which is making her demented," Sophie suggested.

"What the hell are you talking about? That has got to be the stupidest thing I have ever heard."

"Not any stupider than that crap about non-life-threatening things as a sweet resistance fighter." Sophie growled back.

"Ladies! Please! This is not the roller derby or female wrestling! Alice needs her rest and you two are ready to take a swing at one another."

Caitlin shooed them out the door. She turned back to Alice. "Is there anything you need?"

"The last twelve months of my life? If you can't do that, then can I have a glass of water?"

"Sure, I can do that." Caitlin walked out and left Alice alone.

Alice looked out the window. "Twelve months?" she whispered. A strange woman stood in the doorway to her room. "Who are you?"

"My name is Doris and I'm new to the home. I just wanted to see if you were all right." She took a step toward the bed. "Do you want some company?"

Alice wasn't sure what she wanted, so she remained silent. "Do I have to answer right now?" she finally said.

"Fine. Well, I'm a couple of rooms away if you need any assistance."

"Thank you, dear." Alice watched Doris leave. "Dear? I never say dear," she grumbled. She had always thought that 'dear' signified you were old. Was she?

"Here you go." Caitlin appeared with the glass and offered it to her. "Let me help you." She placed her arm around Alice's shoulders and helped her to sit up. The water was cool and wet and soothed her parched lips. When she signaled she had had enough, Caitlin let her back down to the pillow. She left the glass on the bedside table.

Caitlin patted her on the shoulder. "Get some rest."

Alice nodded and closed her eyes.

Chapter Twenty-one

A Quick Dip

As far as Mel was concerned, it had been way too long since she had seen Caitlin. She remembered that kiss in excruciating detail and wanted to experience more. Work had inundated her and she barely had time to make the occasional phone call to see how Alice was. Caitlin was worried, but not to the point that she had to drop everything and drive out. Alice's alter ego slowly re-emerged and after a week she was back to her happy personality. Mel felt it was time to pay a visit.

"Hey there," Mel greeted Caitlin cheerfully.

"What are you doing here?"

"Did I make so little an impression on you? I can't turn up and say hello to my favorite girl?"

Caitlin dipped her head. "Sorry. Come in." She stepped aside and let Mel enter.

"Are you girls doing anything today?"

"Not really, no. Why?"

"Maybe I want to steal you away for an afternoon of naughty delights."

Caitlin blushed.

"But that's not it."

The blush faded just as quickly and was replaced with disappointment.

Mel laughed. "I'll have to remember that. No, I wanted to suggest a picnic... for everyone. I spotted a really nice park the other day, with a duck pond and picnic tables. It even has a swing set for Alice."

"Let me get some lunch together."

"Already done. All I'm waiting on is you." Mel held out her hand and took Caitlin's in her own.

154

Isabel walked to the bookshelf and found a partially-completed crossword puzzle book. "Enjoy yourselves."

Mel glanced at her. "We will. Of course, if you don't want to come along, that's fine." She returned her gaze to Caitlin. "I'm sure the two of us can find something to do… alone."

"So, is that an invite?"

"I thought I was pretty clear. Wasn't I?"

Caitlin shook her head. "The invite is for everyone. Tell them to get a move along. We're going on a picnic." She addressed Mel. "If you'll excuse me—"

"I know where the coffee is." Mel grinned impishly at her. "G'wan." She swatted Caitlin's ass as she turned. "Pack your bikini."

"Do you know what the temperature is outside? What do I need that for?"

"In case you fall into the duck pond."

"Hmmm, I better get a change of clothes for Alice then."

Mel's stare skimmed across Caitlin's receding body, resting for a few moments on her ass. She sighed deeply before wandering into the kitchen. The kettle seemed to take ages to boil, so she poked around Caitlin's inner sanctum, opening cupboards and tins to see what was inside them. Maybe it was more to see how close to poverty they really were. While they weren't 'just surviving' they weren't 'rolling in excess' either. Maybe it was time to do something about that.

Mel was on her second coffee when the ladies appeared. Alice turned up in shorts, shirt and sandals, with a small bucket clasped in her hand. Mel's eyebrow rose and she looked at Caitlin.

"I tried to tell her but she's got it in her head that we're going to the beach."

"Sorry, I'm not driving several hundred miles to indulge a whim. Will she be warm enough?" Alice smiled at her and winked. Mel did a double take and wondered what that wink meant. Mel steered the group out the door, waiting momentarily while Caitlin locked up.

"Where are we going?"

155

"I don't know if you know it. It's on Valiant Drive, about 5 miles away."

"Valiant Drive?" Caitlin paused in thought. "Don't think I know that one."

"We'll use Doris's car for this trip and see if it solves your problem about transport." Mel approached the car and opened the doors for the women to find their seats. She collapsed Phyllis's wheelchair and packed it in what was loosely called the trunk. It amused her to see asses sticking out of the vehicle at all angles as they attempted to climb into the SUV. "Anyone need a hand?"

Just as she reached for Sophie's ass, Caitlin responded, "Uh, uh, uh! Hands off!"

"How am I supposed to help?"

"You don't." Caitlin sidled up next to Mel and whispered, "Besides, you don't want her to get ideas, do you?"

Mel's hands swung away rapidly. "Hell, no!" She'd only just gotten Sophie to back off. Instead, Mel moved around to the other side of the vehicle and offered Isabel a hand. When it looked like everyone was settled, Mel climbed into the driver's seat. "Everyone buckled up?"

"Yes." The response was monotonic and undramatic, and sounded very much like an old school field trip.

The engine turned over with a powerful roar and Mel slipped the gear into drive. She drove carefully down the street until she got used to the car. In her peripheral vision she saw Caitlin scowl.

"What's wrong?"

"Will we get there in an hour?"

Mel felt her own face contort into a matching scowl. She was so tempted to respond sarcastically but she stopped herself. "The sun is out. It's a nice day. Consider this part of the picnic."

"It's like standing in line for the bathroom. Why don't you let me drive? I can get us there in no time."

Her hands tightened on the steering wheel in annoyance.

"Because she wants to get there in one piece," Phyllis answered.

"Is that what you were thinking? I can't believe you'd think that."

"I didn't say anything."

"No, but you were thinking it."

"I was not. Phyllis—"

"Don't drag poor Phyllis into this."

"Bu... I...she...." Mel clamped her lips shut and put her foot to the floor. In her anger she ignored the speed limit and careened down the road as if her ass was on fire. After fifteen minutes of sheer terror, she pulled the SUV into the parking lot of the park. The doors flew open and the women got out as quick as they could. Mel's hands were plastered to the steering wheel.

"See? That didn't take long." Caitlin said cheerily as she unbuckled her seat belt.

Mel's bottom lip quivered.

"What's wrong?" Caitlin reached for Mel's seat belt release. "Come on, let's eat."

Mel knew Caitlin said something, but she just couldn't grasp the words. Her brain swirled in a mass of endorphins and she wasn't quite ready to come down off her 'high' just yet. She tugged at her fingers but they were embedded in the sticky leather.

The driver's side door opened and Alice reached in to gently prise her fingers off. She lent a hand to help Mel onto her feet, and only grabbed hold of her when Mel's legs gave out. When Caitlin disappeared around the back to get Phyllis's wheelchair, Alice pushed her gently down to sit on the grass. "Put your head between your knees," she muttered.

Mel looked up and wondered who she was listening to. Was it the old woman or the resistance fighter? "Who are you?"

"Anyone you want me to be."

"This is all a game, isn't it?"

Alice didn't verbally respond, instead giving Mel a wink and a hearty salute.

"Well, I'll be—"

"What are you sitting down for? We have a picnic to enjoy." Caitlin said as she pushed Phyllis, and the basket on Phyllis's lap, toward the cement picnic table and benches.

Alice extended her hand and Mel allowed herself to be pulled upright. How could such a petite thing be so strong? She decided it must have been all that swinging around earlier in her life. By the time Mel reached the table Caitlin was busy unpacking the basket and handing out napkins. "The food's going to dry out if you wait any longer. Grab a sandwich."

As much as she wanted a stiff drink, Mel settled for one of the cans of soda. She popped the lid and it squirted in all directions, including all over her crisp new shirt.

"It's just not your day," Sophie commented.

She was on the verge of tears. What else could go wrong? In case she choked on her meal, Mel took her camera out of her bag instead. Maybe a photo or two would drive away the bad-luck demon.

"What is that?"

"It's a bar of soap." Mel shook her head in dismay. "What does it look like?"

"It looks like a camera."

"Right. And what do you do with a camera?" Mel asked.

"Eat it?" Caitlin offered before she filled her mouth with the sandwich.

Mel pursed her lips then took a picture of Caitlin with her mouth full. "I'll frame that one." As they ate their meal the sound of quacking ducks filled the air.

"Can I go feed them?" Alice asked.

"Sure. I better go with you." Caitlin snatched another sandwich to take with her, before she strolled down the gently sloping pathway after Alice.

With some amusement Mel watched the two of them walk toward the waiting ducks, at least until Alice spotted the swings and spritely shuffled to them, as only a fourteen-year old girl inside an eighty year old woman can do.

"Alice!"

Mel could hear the frustration in Caitlin's voice from where she was. Alice had them all wrapped around her little finger. If Mel was honest, she'd have to include herself in that number.

Sophie looked at her expectantly.

"Do you want to go see the ducks?" Mel asked, knowing very well that was what Sophie was waiting for her to ask.

"I'd love to."

"Isabel?"

"Why not?"

Mel glanced at Phyllis, but she was engaged in conversation with Doris. "Let's leave them be." She reached into the basket and found some left-over bread, while the camera slid easily into her jeans pocket. Maybe she could take a family photo or two of the ladies. "Can you keep an eye on my bag?" Mel asked Phyllis, but it appeared she wasn't listening. "That's okay. I'll get the seal to look after it."

"Fine," Phyllis responded absently.

"Sheesh," Isabel whispered. "They're making me sick."

"I thought she said nothing was going on." Sophie said.

"Yeah, that's what I thought."

"It appears to be a non-relationship. It's nothing like the relationship you want to have."

Isabel shrugged. "I can't see what all the fuss is about."

"Spoken like a true academic." Sophie studied the two women, hunched close to one another deep in conversation. "You know, I think I get it."

"Good. You can explain it to me."

"I can hear those ducks calling." Mel steered the two women down the path toward the pond.

"They're making an awful racket."

Isabel elaborated, "In fact, one sounds like a woman screaming."

Mel caught the movement in her peripheral vision and watched in awe as Phyllis flew by them in her wheelchair, her echoing yells of joy fading away as she sped down the hill. When she heard, "Oh, shit!" Mel ran after her.

She arrived as Phyllis splashed about in the pond. Quickly, she reached into her pocket and started snapping pictures. The camera bobbed about as Mel tried to hold her laughter in check. Phyllis finally surfaced under a large lily pad. Water spouted out of her mouth, casually arcing back into the pond. A noisy quack made her look up and she found herself nose to beak with a duck, who was gazing at her upside down from its position on top of the lily pad on her head.

Mel kept her finger down on the button and the camera whirred crazily as it took picture after picture.

"If you don't stop taking those damned photos I may just have to do something about it."

"Where's your sense of humor?" Mel took a step back in case Phyllis got any ideas.

"Back at the top of the hill. That god-be-damned chair broke. The insurance company is trying to short-change me." When no one moved to help, Phyllis yelled, "Get me the hell out of here!"

The volume was enough for the duck to jump off in disgust and swim to the other side of the pond. However it didn't leave without an angry quack or two, and a quick poke with its beak on Phyllis's arm.

"You sure know how to make friends." Mel chuckled. She looked down at her clothes and wondered how she could salvage them if she went in to save Phyllis. When she made a move to remove her sandshoes Alice waded in, oblivious of the water, the mud and her clothes.

"Alice!"

"Did you bring that change of clothes?" Mel asked.

"Yes, I did, but not a towel."

Doris finally reached the bottom of the incline. "Is she all right?"

"Nothing's hurt except her pride." Mel thought it was cute when Doris fussed around on the bank. She left them and trudged back up the hill to the car to find the small bundle of clothes Caitlin had brought. She carried it down to the waiting group on the pond bank. "I think I should dash back to the house and get some towels."

"Probably a good idea. Here." Caitlin reached into her pocket and took out her keys. She separated them out and handed her the key ring, holding the one key to the front door. "This one."

"Where are the towels?"

"Closet, outside the bathroom."

"Will you be okay?"

"Sure. Always have been."

But Mel wasn't convinced. Caitlin sounded tired—or resigned—she couldn't tell which. "I won't be long."

It was nice to travel back to the house at her own speed. Despite the urgency, Mel didn't want to experience the terror of driving like Nascar again anytime soon, even though it was in the cards that the return trip with everyone in the vehicle would result in just that.

Mel found the towels easily and was tempted to get a change of clothes for Phyllis as well, but poking around in Phyllis's personal things was probably overstepping her role as the taxi driver. Instead, she grabbed another towel for good measure.

By the time she returned, the women were congregated around the picnic table. The remnants of the meal had been cleared and Caitlin looked like she was impatient to get home. She was not going to argue with a woman on the verge of a meltdown.

As she packed away the wheelchair into the car she checked it. "What happened?"

"Damned brakes didn't hold."

Mel fiddled with the small handle that pushed a metal bar against the wheel. While it held the wheel when a little pressure was applied, it quickly released when the pressure increased. "You'll need to call the insurance company."

"No shit!"

"Phyllis! No cussing!"

"Then tell the Mistress of Understatement here to stop saying stupid things."

"Phyllis! Enough!" Caitlin rubbed her forehead. "You apologize."

Phyllis sighed. "Sorry, Doc. If I'd have known how much trouble this thing was to replace I wouldn't have sat out on the sidewalk in the first place."

"That seems like years ago." Mel remembered only too well the terrifying trip Phyllis took down the road behind a speeding removal truck.

Phyllis wiggled her middle finger. "Not that long ago. Damned thing still aches."

Mel finally sat behind the steering wheel and took a deep breath. Despite Caitlin's constant urging, she managed to keep her emotions under control and the car travelling along at the speed limit. When the car finally pulled up in the driveway of the home Mel felt pleased with herself. She had managed to resist Caitlin's badgering and drove the way she wanted to.

"Come on. Everyone inside." Mel handed Caitlin the keys to the house and watched from the driver's seat as she ushered the women in.

Caitlin stuck her head out the door. "Are you coming?"

She felt exhausted. Not physically, but emotionally. Now she remembered why she wasn't in a steady relationship. It was hard work. Mel got out of the car and locked up, trudging wearily inside the house.

Chapter Twenty-two

One More Step

"Do you feel better?" Doris asked as Phyllis emerged from the bathroom.

"Tired. Do you know how hard it is to get wet clothing off?" Phyllis glared at Sophie. "Don't you say a word!"

Sophie lifted a hand to her mouth and made a zipper motion.

Alice cheerfully jogged down the hall, a silly grin plastered on her face. "Well, that was exciting." She saluted Caitlin. "I'll patrol the perimeter, Captain. Make sure we're all safe." Alice then saluted Mel. "Major..."

"Nothing fazes her, eh?"

"Nothing that I've found so far," Caitlin answered. "Except for getting lost."

"That was a momentary lapse. She seems as cheerful as ever." She drew her gaze back to the remaining women. "So, what are we going to do this afternoon?"

"I'm kind of tired," Sophie responded before adding a wide yawn. "I think I'll take a nap."

"Maybe we all should make use of this time to rest."

Mel wondered what had exhausted Caitlin that she needed a rest. The woman seemed to have limitless energy, or so she thought.

"Are you all right?"

"Yeah. Just a bit of a headache."

"That's the second one in the last few days. Do these happen often?" Mel felt herself slip into professional mode.

"A bit more lately." Caitlin swiped her hand over her brow.

"Wait a moment." Mel disappeared outside and returned a minute later with her medical bag.

"I'm fine. I don't need—"

"Let me examine you."

"What?"

"As a physician, of course."

Caitlin's eyes widened. "Here?" Her voice rose to a tight squeak.

"Your bedroom." Mel said in a low voice. When Caitlin twitched Mel laughed.

"They'll talk."

"So long that's all they do. Lead on."

Reluctantly Caitlin walked down the hall, closely followed by Mel. Mel felt a jolt of excitement when the door closed behind her.

"The inner sanctum, huh?"

Mel looked around the small room. There seemed so little to represent Caitlin's life. She, herself, had her life spread on every inch of her apartment, lazily sprawled wherever it landed. A sudden rush of guilt hit her. She really should clean up her own place... just in case visitors ever visited. Not that she can remember friends visiting in recent memory, but she had put that down to her profession. Was it because she lived in a pigsty?

"Mel?"

Her attention immediately turned to Caitlin and she gave her a wide grin.

"What's that smile for?"

"That's the first time you've ever called me Mel."

"No, it's not."

"Oh, yes, it is," Mel said confidently. "And it sounds great."

Perched on the edge of the mattress, Caitlin's finger traced the pattern on her bedspread. "I thought you were the doctor and I was the patient."

"We can play that game if you want. Now let's see..." Mel opened her bag and slung her stethoscope around her neck. "Where does it hurt?" She wiggled her eyebrows.

"Headache, Doc," Caitlin reminded her.

"Ah, yes." Mel cleared her throat and put her professional demeanor back in place. "How long have you had these headaches?"

"Last few months."

Mel breathed out forcefully. At least it didn't start when Doris entered the house. "Things getting a little too much for you?"

"No more than usual."

Mel found her flashlight and shone it in Caitlin's eyes. Each pupil contracted as it should have. "Any specific time of day?"

"Mainly afternoons, sometimes after dinner."

"Hmmm."

"What does 'hmmm' mean?" Caitlin asked nervously.

"For now, just hmmm."

"Did you hear something?"

✝

"What are you doing?" Isabel stood in the doorway to her room watching Sophie standing next to Caitlin's bedroom door.

"Sshhhh." The actual sound was loud and harsh, and defeated the purpose of the reminder to be quiet.

"What's going on?"

"Will you keep it down!"

Isabel approached Sophie and leaned down to the doorknob. "What am I listening for?"

"Caitlin and the doc are in there… alone."

"No kidding?"

"What are you doing?" Suddenly Phyllis appeared in the hallway.

"Caitlin and the doc," Sophie said excitedly, her finger pointing at Caitlin's door.

"It's none of your business."

"Well said, Phyllis." Doris added.

"Is this a convention or something?"

"Are we preparing for war?" Finally, the ensemble was complete with the arrival of Alice.

"Will…you…keep…it….down!" Sophie whispered harshly. "I can't hear what's going on."

165

The door suddenly flew open. "And you won't either." Mel, a cranky expression in place, stood there with her hands on her hips. She waited for Isabel to straighten up and step away.

"How did you hear us?"

"A deaf man two blocks away could have heard you. Just what do you think you're doing?"

"Errr...." Sophie searched for an excuse. "I thought I heard someone cry out. I was hopeful that I'd at least get to hear what all the commotion about lesbian sex was."

Mel looked at Isabel "I was coming to Sophie's aid."

"I can't remember what sex is."

"And what about you two?" Mel asked of Phyllis.

"We had nothing to do with this. They started it."

"Oh, and if I wasn't here you'd be—"

"Enough! Nothing is going on, all right? Caitlin is not feeling well and I was examining her."

"Hee hee," Sophie chuckled. "That's more like it. Playing doctors and nurses."

"No wonder she's getting headaches. You lot are always making snide remarks."

"Doc, in case you haven't noticed, it's all we've got. We're too old for anything else."

"Speak for yourself."

"Alice, you are an exception in anyone's book." Mel commented. "Caitlin is stressed out. Can't you keep it down just for a little while?"

"Of course, you have the perfect prescription for relaxation."

"I would prescribe some Tylenol."

"That's the wimp's way out." Sophie's lips curled upward. "I was thinking of something a little more hands on."

"Stop that right now!" Mel's voice hardened. "That sort of thing is her business."

"It should be yours, Doc," Phyllis answered.

"Phyllis!" Doris looked shocked at the comment.

"Close the door." Phyllis indicated the door in question with her head. When Mel complied, she continued, "It's about time you took action, Doc. A kiss is a good start, but she's not going to wait around for you forever."

"I don't need any help from you."

"Someone's gotta help you. You are way too slow."

"She hasn't indicated—"

"She won't, Doc. You're the one who will have to make the move."

"But—"

"No buts, Doc. You're wasting time standing here talking to us." Phyllis waved her hands at Mel, effectively shooing her out of the hallway. "Go."

"But—"

"Come on, girls. It's a nice sunny day outside. Let's give them some privacy."

"But…" Sophie muttered as she walked away disappointed.

Phyllis raised her thumb and gave her a sign of approval as Mel opened the door and disappeared inside to Caitlin's bedroom.

†

"What was that all about?"

"You don't want to know."

"If I didn't want to know I wouldn't have asked."

Mel studied Caitlin's cranky expression. "Phyllis was telling me to 'go for it'."

"Go for what?"

"Caitlin, are you that innocent?"

"I am not!" she said indignantly. "I know what she means."

"It doesn't matter whether you do or not."

"So, are you going for it?" Caitlin gave Mel a shy smile, making Mel laugh out loud.

"I thought you had a headache."

"I do." Caitlin's forehead creased.

"Then *it* can wait." Mel dug around in her bag and brought out a pill bottle. She opened it and shook out a couple of tablets. "Take these and get some rest."

167

Caitlin took the pills and looked up at Mel. "Will you stay?"

"If you want. Aren't you worried they'll think we've been having sex?" Mel saw Caitlin wince.

"But we won't be."

"That's beside the point. We're in here and unless you invite in an observer they will think what they will think."

Caitlin rubbed her hand across her forehead.

"Don't worry about it." Mel slipped off her shoes and sat gently on the bed. She handed Caitlin the glass of water sitting on her bedside table and watched as Caitlin swallowed the two pills. "Now, get some rest."

"What about the others?" Caitlin said, even as she closed her eyes.

"Let me take care of it."

"Don't leave." Caitlin's hand slipped across the bedcovers and wrapped around Mel's wrist.

"I won't." Gently, Mel lowered herself to the bed. "Come here." She pulled Caitlin into her arms and felt the body lying on her slowly relax. She stayed that way until Caitlin's breath became steady and even.

Mel indulged herself with a look down Caitlin's sleeping body. Her gaze hesitated at her face and took in the soft skin, arched eyebrows and silky hair. She felt her heart skip a beat. The woman was so darned cute and she couldn't stop herself from smiling.

Her finger rose and ran gently down Caitlin' cheek, stopping momentarily at her lips. Caitlin stirred and her tongue emerged to swipe her lips and Mel's finger. Another twitch sent her heart rate up a notch.

Mel waited for Caitlin to settle before she slowly removed herself from the embrace. She sat on the edge of the bed and looked down at the sleeping woman. With a sigh, Mel stood and collected her bag and shoes. Before she could change her mind, she opened the door and left Caitlin to sleep.

She found the women out on the back patio, as Phyllis had promised.

168

"That was quick." Sophie shifted in her seat. "I thought you said it takes a long time."

"Nothing happened. She was exhausted and needed some sleep." Mel glared at Phyllis. "And I'd like to keep it that way."

"I'm telling you, Doc. You're missing a golden opportunity."

"Well, as the saying goes, 'it ain't over till the fat lady sings'."

"I hope you're not referring to me!" Sophie huffed.

"What were you ladies talking about?"

"Caitlin's birthday."

"Really? When is it?"

"Yesterday. We wanted to get her a present, but it's a bit hard when she's always with us. Besides, she has our money."

Mel thought for a moment. "How about I pick up something for you? You can pay me back later. What did you have in mind?"

"We wanted to get her a new pair of slippers," Isabel piped in, "but we don't know her shoe size."

"That's easy enough solved. Where are her old ones?"

Isabel looked at Phyllis, who replied, "In her bedroom."

"Oh."

"Who wants to volunteer to go in?" Phyllis looked from one woman to the next. Before she had finished silently questioning two of them, Alice stood up and left.

"Oh, no. No, no, no. Alice!" Mel whispered harshly. Before she could stop her Alice opened Caitlin's door and fell to the floor, crossing the carpet like she was a combatant in no-man's land trying to get to a machine gun nest. Wide-eyed, Mel watched her circle the bed and grab one of the dowdy slippers on the far side of the room. She cringed when Alice put the slipper in her mouth to free up both hands to crawl back.

"Did you have to do that?" Mel mentally spit out bits of material from her mouth. The sight of the slipper dangling from Alice's teeth was just too much to handle. Alice, on the other hand, didn't even blink when she removed it from her mouth.

"Mission accomplished, major." She seemed inordinately pleased with herself as she handed over the soggy slipper. "Now what?"

"Now," Phyllis said as she sidled up next to Mel with a pen and paper, "we trace the shoe and go shopping."

Mel shuddered at the thought of taking five elderly hellions to the mall. One she could handle, or maybe even two, but five was beyond her comprehension. "Sorry, girls. I'm not as good at multitasking as Caitlin is. I can take two of you." She couldn't bear to see the crestfallen faces so she moved to grab her bag. "Alice, you're one."

"Awww," Sophie whined.

"Do you want me to leave Alice here for you to look after?"

"She has a point."

"I'll go," Isabel piped in before anyone else could speak.

"Let's go." Mel reached for the front door and waited for the two women to leave.

"What if she wakes up?"

Mel looked at Sophie. "Then say hello. It's not like she's a prisoner or something."

"Do we tell her where you've gone?"

"Tell her we've gone out to get some dinner. Don't mention her birthday."

"And?"

"And don't let her pick up a pot. Coffee-making is fine, by the way, but no cooking. Got it?" Mel looked at Sophie, Phyllis and Doris and patiently waited for some sort of affirmation that they understood.

Alice bounded toward Mel's car while Mel and Isabel took a more casual stroll. "Where's the nearest mall?"

"Let's see..." Isabel thought about it as she made herself comfortable in the back seat.

"Are we going to Berlin?" Alice asked excitedly.

"No, I thought we'd go to Paris."

"Is that a good idea telling her that?"

Mel opened her mouth then thought better of saying what was sitting on the tip of her tongue. She didn't want to hex herself by saying 'what could possibly go wrong?' With Alice added to the mix, possibly everything could go wrong. Now she had second thoughts about bringing her along.

"So, where are we going?" Mel grabbed the steering wheel and looked into the rear view mirror at Isabel seated in the back.

"I know there's one around here somewhere." Isabel tapped her teeth.

"Fine." Mel took out her cell and brought up the map app. After some searching she found a suitable mall a few miles away. She tried to memorize the directions and hoped that they reached their intended target some time before dusk.

"Give it to me," Isabel offered.

Mel handed her the phone. "Can you see it?"

"I'm old, not blind."

"I hate to tell you, Isabel, but those two things are mutually exclusive, along with deafness and dementia."

"I ain't got dementia." Alice said.

"Sure you don't, honey." Mel patted Alice's leg.

"Don't be condescending," Alice snapped.

Mel blinked.

"What did she say?"

"Errr, nothing. Let's go get some presents."

Regardless of the possibility of ending up in another county, city or state, Mel managed to find the mall she was looking for. They scoured the parking lot for a spot to park. Despite it being Saturday afternoon, the mall was busy. Finally she found a spot so far away that she wondered if it were easier to have walked from the home. All three were sweating freely by the time they reached the entrance to the mall.

Mel breathed deeply as the air conditioning hit her. "Map, map, map," she muttered absently as she looked for an information board. "There." She didn't wait for Alice or Isabel to join her. Her finger ran down the list of shops until she found what she was looking for. "Now, girls…" Mel looked around and was surprised to find the two women still standing at the door. "Come on. Let's go shopping!"

Normally shopping was something that she had to do to eat or be well dressed for work. It wasn't exactly a chore, but it wasn't a delight either. Shopping took energy and usually by the time she got around to getting into her car her energy was nearly non-existent. This time was no different, but having two potential escapees nearby she knew she had to be on her toes. What on earth made her decide to bring them along? Oh yeah, birthday present. She wanted the present to be bought by *them*, not leaving them as middle-women in a line of three.

"Ooohh, look at this!" Alice's eyes grew wide as she stared into a jeweler's window. "That's nice." She pointed out a pendant that took her fancy.

"You can't afford it." Mel noted the twelve-hundred-dollar price tag.

"You can."

"No, I can't."

"Sure, you can," Isabel said. "Caitlin would really love it."

"I don't know her well enough to give her that."

"What are you talking about?"

""It's too personal for someone I barely know."

"That's silly." Alice scowled at Mel. "Is it some sort of protocol?"

"Not as such. If I gave her that it would mean two things. Firstly, she would feel embarrassed about getting something so expensive from me when she has no chance of returning the favor."

"You'd expect something like that?" Mel knew she had fallen in Alice's expectations.

"Of course not, but the guilt would be there. Besides, giving something like that would escalate the relationship."

"Escalate? I don't understand."

Mel's gaze swept across the pendant. It was a really nice piece of jewelry and she would love to give it to Caitlin, but it would only cause trouble. "That's more for 'will you move in with me', or 'will you marry me'. It's not for a first 'happy birthday'."

"How about here?" Alice had already moved on to the next store. Mel looked down the long corridor at the myriad of store fronts that lay ahead and sighed deeply. It was going to be a long afternoon.

Chapter Twenty-three

Happy Birthday

Caitlin woke to an empty room. She had hoped that Mel would have stayed with her, but she knew it was wishful thinking at best. Her headache had receded and, while not gone, it was noticeably less than what it was. Maybe she needed a holiday. As if.

Reluctantly Caitlin got up off the bed and found her shoes, slipping them on before she opened the door. It was quiet. Too quiet. "Hello?" she asked tentatively.

"You're up."

Caitlin heard the voice and knew it to be Phyllis. At least someone was home.

"Where is everyone?"

"The doc has gone shopping. She took Alice and Isabel with her. Sophie's trying to draw something. I don't think I want to know what it is."

"It's not that bad, is it?"

"Actually, she draws quite well. It's the subject matter I'm worried about, if you get my drift." Phyllis wheeled her old chair closer to Caitlin. "Are you sure you can't afford a computer? At least the body parts are roughly in proportion on the porn sites."

"Ewww." Caitlin's headache reared its ugly head. She felt a nerve twitch around her temple.

Phyllis chuckled. "I'm kidding. She's drawing fruit. At least, that's what she told me."

Caitlin rubbed the patch of skin that twitched. "You are going to be the death of me."

"Relax."

Caitlin walked past Phyllis muttering under her breath. Phyllis wheeled around and followed her. "What are you doing?"

"Firstly, I'm going to make a cup of coffee then I have to think about dinner. Did Doctor Stokes say whether she's eating with us?"

"You can make the coffee, but you have to step away from the vegetables."

"Why? Are they going to explode?"

"If you touch them, they might."

"What's going on?" Caitlin stood there with her hands on her hips. "I'm not in the mood for word games."

"The doc said she'll pick up something for dinner and told me to stop you from cooking."

"I'm not that bad."

"It wasn't a comment on your cooking skills. She thought you deserved a break."

"Oh. In that case, that's nice." Caitlin made her coffee then sat down at the kitchen table. Her fingers drummed the table top. "Where's Doris?"

"She's taking a nap."

"Coffee?"

"Sure."

While Caitlin made the coffee Phyllis found the cookie jar. Finally they sat across from one another sipping their coffee. "Why is Mel doing this?"

"I don't know. Maybe it's the headache and all, and she's trying to ease your workload."

Caitlin's eyebrow rose. "Workload?"

"Give you a break from cooking."

"I know what workload means. I was wondering why you were using the word."

"I can occasionally come up with a fancy word or two when I need to."

Phyllis sounded offended but Caitlin ignored it. She was too tired to worry about bruised egos. "Did she say when she'd be back?"

"Missing her already?" Phyllis grinned as she reached into the jar and grabbed herself a cookie.

"I want to know when I should think about calling the cops about three missing women."

"You could always call her," Phyllis said matter-of-factly.

"Oh. I hadn't thought of that." She noticed that Phyllis quickly filled her mouth with coffee, probably to stop a pithy comment passing her lips.

Phyllis looked at her watch. "I wouldn't panic yet."

"What time did they leave?"

"A couple of hours ago. Remember, she's got Alice with her."

"What on earth possessed her to take her?"

"She was worried about leaving us to look after her."

So far, she couldn't fault Mel's thoughtfulness. Despite her anxiety, she stopped herself from reaching for her cell. She would wait.

†

The car pulled up in front of the home and Mel finally felt her tension ease. It had been one hell of an afternoon. She turned off the engine and faced her two passengers. "Okay. This is what we'll do. For the moment we'll only take in the birthday card and the games. Alice, this is top secret. Okay? Once I have Caitlin distracted, Isabel you get everyone to sign the card then come out to the car and get the slippers. You got that?"

"I'll need the key."

"Everyone out." Mel hopped out of the car and helped Isabel out of the back seat. She didn't worry about Alice because the woman beat her to the sidewalk before she'd even closed her own door. Everyone got to carry some packages. It was something like Christmas all over again. In fact, it was exactly like Christmas, at least for these little old ladies. She pushed the button on her key ring and heard the satisfying beep of the car locking. "Push this button. It will unlock the car. To lock it, press it again. Any questions?"

"Nope." Isabel took the keys and put them in her pants pocket.

Mel took a deep breath. "Okay, here goes." She waited for Alice and Isabel to enter the house before she stepped inside. Caitlin's voice dashed her hopes that she had a bit of respite before the birthday bash began.

"How did it go? What have you got there?"

"Good. Just a few items you had listed on the refrigerator. I didn't think you'd get the chance anytime soon. Once Alice spotted the toy store there was no stopping her."

"I thought you were gone a long time just for dinner."

Dinner? Mel slapped her forehead. "I knew there was something else."

"Else? That's all you had to pick up."

"Besides these." Mel shook the parcels in her hand.

"I didn't know about them."

Mel had to think on her feet. Out of the corner of her eye she saw Isabel signal to Phyllis. "Cut me some slack. I had Alice with me. She wanted to look in every store we passed. After a while they all looked the same and I'd forgotten what I was there for."

Caitlin studied her and she began to shift under her gaze.

"What do you feel like? Pizza, fried chicken, Chinese?"

"I try to provide healthy meals."

Mel's eyebrow rose. "And all those cookies?"

"Fiber."

Mel laughed. "If that's how you want to look at it. How about we go out for dinner?"

Caitlin's eyes widened. "We've never gone out for dinner before."

"All the more reason that we do."

"It's too early though."

"I suppose we'll have to find something to do to fill in the time." Mel looked pointedly at Caitlin, who blushed. "My, my, such a mind." She laughed harder. "Now you have all those new games to play we can start there."

"Thank you for that. I *will* repay you."

"I know you will. Did you receive the winnings?"

"Yeah. In fact, the check cleared the bank two days ago. We'd sat down and made a list of stuff. I was wondering when I could go shopping. Thank you for sharing the load."

"My pleasure. Alice got such a kick out of spending the money. She said she was tired of rations out of a tin and scrounging around for toilet paper."

"Oh, God, she didn't!"

"Yep, the sales assistant didn't know where to look. That might explain why he took a step or two back when handling the merchandise." Mel chuckled as she remembered the visible wince on his face. "We did add one or two things to the list before we left."

"I can't afford…"

"Don't you worry about it. It was something the girls wanted to do. Isabel!" she yelled. "Are you ready?"

"Yeah, Doc."

The five women came into the kitchen, making the room feel crowded and stuffy.

"Happy birthday!" they all yelled at once.

"Sorry, it's not wrapped."

"We didn't have time." Mel added. "I had a tough enough time getting them to decide on the slippers. I didn't want to cause World War Three because of wrapping paper."

"World War… Three?" Alice's eyes widened. "I must prepare."

"Alice!" Mel called. "It's a joke. There is no World War Three."

"Major, that is not funny."

"Open it," Sophie asked excitedly.

"Will you look at that!" Caitlin said. "They're wonderful."

Mel didn't miss the slight wince. "Plaid was all they had in your size."

"Just what I wanted. Thank you all so much." Caitlin gave each woman an enthusiastic hug. When she ended up in front of Mel, she smiled sweetly. "Thank you for helping them. It was very thoughtful."

177

"Here you go, Doc." Isabel handed her the flowers.

"These are for you," Mel said. "I felt I couldn't go wrong with these."

"Unless she was allergic to them."

"Phyllis, hush. That is sooo sweet." Caitlin smelled the blooms and her smile rose to her eyes.

Phyllis nudged Mel. "Looks like you're in."

Mel's mouth opened and closed. "I don't know what I can say to that. That's not what I intended."

"I'm sure you didn't, at least not in front of all these witnesses. Oh, and everyone?" Caitlin added, "The doctor has offered to take us all out for dinner. How about that?"

"That's great!"

"Real dinner? Like sitting down and stuff?"

"Yes," Mel responded, "we actually get to stay and eat at a table. You can even use the bathroom there. If you're real good they might give you some cutlery."

"Oh, hush," Doris snorted.

"We've got some new table games. Go find one that we can all play." Mel ushered them out of the kitchen. "Meanwhile, we'll make some coffee."

Phyllis poked her head in. "Does the meal include alcohol?"

"Sure does." Mel chuckled when she saw Phyllis grin widely.

Caitlin filled the kettle and put it on to boil. Mel stood by and watched her. She fiddled with her jeans pocket and bit her bottom lip.

"Thank you for taking them out. It was a great surprise."

"It's sad to think that your birthday could have gone by unnoticed."

"They knew when it was but there wasn't much opportunity for them to do anything. I'm indebted to you for making them happy."

"And you? Are you happy?" Mel shifted closer.

"Of course. Why do you ask?"

"Nothing, really. I was just curious." Mel's hand slipped into her pocket and she took out a small bag. "This is for you."

Caitlin looked up from the bag to Mel's eyes. "What's this?"

"It's a bag with a box inside. What does it look like?"

"Can't you be serious for one moment?"

"Happy birthday," Mel murmured quietly.

"I thought the flowers—"

"That was an appetizer. This is the main dish." Mel withdrew her hand when Caitlin's fingers brushed her skin. "Open it."

She watched intently as Caitlin seemed to take forever to take out the box. The inhale of breath was a good sign, or so she thought. The single tear that rolled down Caitlin's cheek when she opened the box sealed the deal. It seemed she liked it.

"Wow," Caitlin whispered. "That is beautiful."

"Here, let me." Mel took the pendant gently from Caitlin's hands and proceeded to place it around her neck. Her fingers brushed the soft skin of Caitlin's neck and her response didn't go unnoticed.

"You shouldn't have." Caitlin's fingers rose to caress the small silver heart dangling from the chain.

"I was going to buy you a coffee maker, but Alice convinced me to buy this."

"A coffee maker?"

"I know. It's a little impersonal, but I thought this may have been too much too soon."

"Too soon for what?"

Mel saw the confusion written on Caitlin's face. She took a moment to order her thoughts. "I know we haven't known one another long. Pretty short really. I thought that the pendant was maybe saying more than you were ready to hear. I wanted to get you something for your birthday, and since you are trying to kill us all with coffee I thought a coffee maker was a safe bet."

"What changed your mind?" The kettle boiled and Caitlin set about making the coffee.

"Alice. She said if I kept going as slow as I was she'd be dead before I even get to the pendant stage of courting."

"Courting?" Caitlin laughed. "There's a pendant stage?"

"Yeah, courting. I began to wonder whether she was channeling Mary Antoinette or something. There isn't a pendant stage in any relationship book I know of, but I knew what she meant. I figured I couldn't let her die without seeing that."

"Hey, you two! Save the mushy stuff for after we've gone to bed!"

"No! I want to see!"

"Sophie, sit your ass down!"

Mel looked at Caitlin and they both laughed. "I don't think we have any say in this anymore."

"I think you're right." Caitlin lifted three mugs and carried them out the door. Mel followed closely behind with four. "I thought you only had six mugs."

"I had to dip into my 'do not break glass until emergency' collection. Beautiful, don't you think?"

The mug was really ugly. It had chips out of the rim and there was a crack in the glaze down one side.

"No wonder you don't use this one. I only hope it makes it to the table."

"It's got a cup or two left in it. I really should get some new ones."

"Add it to the list."

"And that list is getting longer and longer every day."

Mel slowed her walk down to tiny steps as she tried not to spill the coffee. She didn't feel confident about her waitressing skills and she had to stop mid-way to lighten her load. It was then she knew she'd never make it in the hospitality industry.

✝

Five hours later they returned to the house, exhausted but pleasantly filled. Caitlin watched her charges trudge up the hallway to their rooms.

"Hey, the night's not finished yet."

"For them it is. Coffee?"

Mel smiled. She knew the question was coming even before Caitlin opened her mouth. "Please," she said sweetly.

She heard the clatter of the kettle as it was put on the stove. "What did you have in mind?"

"Huh?" Mel drew herself back from her daydreaming.

"You said the night's not finished. What did you mean?"

Mel joined her in the kitchen and moved to the refrigerator. "No birthday is complete without...," she pulled out a cardboard box, "... a birthday cake." Mel found a plate and put the cake on it, placing two brand-new candles in the middle. "Matches?"

Caitlin walked to a far cupboard and poked around the back of it. "I think... ahhh." She pulled out a matchbox and tossed it across the room. "Don't tell Alice I have those."

"Why don't you want me to include them in the celebration?"

"They're tired," Caitlin said, "even you could see that. There's always lunch tomorrow."

"True, but I'd miss out."

"You're busy?"

"Well, no, but I didn't want to assume that I'd be invited."

"I think you know better."

"Maybe. I think I'm a little insecure about... us."

Caitlin pushed the mug over and waited for Mel to light the candles.

"Happy birthday to you," Mel began to sing. She kept the song to a mere whisper in deference to the others, and somehow it made the moment seem so much more intimate. She gazed in Caitlin's eyes as she continued to sing and saw the sweet response there. "Blow out the candles and make a wish."

Caitlin's gaze never left hers as the candles were extinguished.

"What did you wish for?"

Caitlin didn't say a word, but Mel could see her feelings in her eyes.

"Cut the cake."

Caitlin cut two wafer-thin slices and passed one on a plate. Mel looked at it.

"Do you want more?"

It was a loaded question and Mel was pushed to keep her answer referring to the cake. "Let's see how this goes." She broke off a piece and put it in her mouth, hoping that having her mouth full would stop any errant comment from coming out.

Finally the piece of cake had been eaten and the coffee drunk. Mel had nothing else to keep her there. "I suppose I better go."

"Okay." Caitlin stood and escorted Mel to the door.

"Well, then," Mel said awkwardly. "Goodnight." She didn't want to say goodnight but she felt she had pushed the matter as far as she could. It was now all up to Caitlin. When she didn't respond Mel took a step outside. "I'll see you tomorrow."

Caitlin's mouth opened and closed, as if she was trying to decide whether say something or not. "Stay."

Mel nearly missed the whispered word. She looked at her and wondered whether she had imagined it. "Stay?" she repeated.

"Stay."

"Are you sure?"

"No."

"Don't feel you have to—" But she hoped to God that she did.

Caitlin extended her hand. "Stay."

Without another word, Caitlin locked the door behind Mel and led her down the hallway to her bedroom. Shyly she allowed Mel to enter then followed quietly behind her before closing the door.

Little did either of them know that another bedroom door had opened and an aged face smiled at the turn of events. The door closed with a mere whisper and the silence reigned over the household for the rest of the night.

Chapter Twenty-four

The Final Frontier

"Hey, Doc, what are you doing here so early?" Phyllis looked at the crumple-dressed woman leaning against the sink drinking her ever-present cup of coffee. "What's going on?" She looked from Mel to Caitlin then back to Mel. "Oh. Why didn't someone tell me?"

"For one, it was a spur of the moment thing. Second, we didn't want eavesdroppers listening to every sound coming out of that room."

"We wouldn't do that," Phyllis said indignantly.

"You already had!" Mel replied. "We were nervous as it was. We didn't need people on the bleachers cheering us on."

"Awww, that is so damned cute!"

"What is?" Sophie entered the kitchen and yawned loudly. "What's going on? Doc? What are you doing here at...," Sophie looked at the clock on the wall. "...Six a.m. wearing the clothes that you wore last ni...ahhhh, I see. Oh, bugger, I missed it!"

"No cussing," Caitlin said timidly.

"Miss what?" Isabel strode into the kitchen like she hadn't gone to sleep. "What happened?"

"Caitlin and the doc carried on partying last night after we went to bed."

"Phyllis!"

"Caitlin!" Isabel responded. "About bloody time."

"Isabel!"

Mel stood by and watched the interaction with some amusement.

"You've got nothing to say?" Caitlin pleaded.

"Nope." Mel took another sip of her coffee. "You're doing fine all by yourself."

"Oh, hell!"

"Language!" Phyllis gleefully replied. "No, really… we are very happy for you both. I hope you know that."

"Yeah," Mel sniggered, watching the gathering storm clouds on Caitlin's brow. "Yeah, I know that. Now would be a good time to drop it before we all get kicked out of this place."

Phyllis glanced at a cranky Caitlin. "I think you're right."

"And as much as I'd like to stick around, I have a pigsty called my apartment that I really have to clean."

"Oh."

"I know you're disappointed, but I'm running out of clothes for work. I'm sure my patients would appreciate me fully clothed and smelling like a rose." Mel washed out her mug and put it on the draining board. "I tell you what. I'll call you at lunch when I have a better idea of how much needs to be done." She stepped close and planted a kiss on Caitlin's cheek.

"Oooooooh." There was a chorus of girlish calls as the kiss finished.

"Grow up," Caitlin growled.

"Temper, temper." Phyllis turned her wheelchair around. "C'mon girls, let's set the table for breakfast."

Mel closed the front door behind her and was glad to be out of the house of bickering women. She felt some sympathy for Caitlin, who would have to face the constant teasing, and only hoped she would be welcomed back the next time she showed up.

†

"Are you sure you're ready for this?"

Doris looked at her friend and took a deep breath. "I don't think so, but putting it off is not going to make it go away."

"Good on you."

"Maybe you could tell her?"

"That's not how it works. Sandra will just tell me to butt out. It's between you two."

184

"I know. I don't know what to say to her."

The knock on the front door made Doris jump. Her heart thumped wildly as she contemplated what was to come.

"Be strong." Phyllis gave her the 'thumbs up' and wheeled her chair toward the back door. Doris nodded nervously while she rubbed her sweaty palms down her pants.

As expected, Sandra stood in the doorway until Caitlin stood aside and let her enter.

"Mother," Sandra said cautiously.

"Come on." Caitlin said then ushered the other women out of the room to the backyard. Phyllis hesitated.

"Go on," Doris said quietly, "I'll be fine."

"If you need me…" Phyllis nodded in the direction of Sandra.

"I will." Doris watched Phyllis leave then turned her attention to her daughter. "Sit."

"What's this all about?"

"I think you know."

"If I did, do you think I'd be asking?"

Doris bristled at Sandra's casual dismissal. "Stop these games!"

"Let's get on with this. I have things to do."

"I bet you do."

"What is that supposed to mean? What is the matter with you?"

"I suppose the matter is that I found out about the bank, Sandra. Care to explain?"

Sandra sat there for a moment staring at her. "It was a loan. I'd gotten into serious trouble and I needed the money quickly."

"And you didn't ask me? What did you need it for?"

"The loan. It got on top of me."

"You'd told me it was all taken care of."

"I lied. The repayments were too much."

"I know the loan was for two hundred thousand dollars. What was the extra fifty thousand for?"

"There was the bank interest on the loan."

"Did you pay back anything at all? Did you ever intend to?"

"Of course I intended to! Things got tight with work and I couldn't spare the money. It was the only way to get the bank off my back. At least I saved your house."

"So you are justifying stealing it by saying that you did me a favor saving my own home?"

"I wasn't stealing."

"It would have been a loan if I knew about it, otherwise it's stealing."

"You weren't using it."

"Sandra! Are you listening to yourself?"

"Daddy would have given it to me in his will. Don't you want to honor his wishes?"

"If he had intended to give that amount of money then why did he leave everything to me? Your manipulation of me stops here."

"What do you care? You never cared before. Daddy had to make all the decisions for you."

"And you think you can just step into his shoes, eh? I'm not an idiot."

Sandra said nothing.

"Well, that says a lot," Doris said. "For your information, your father didn't give me the opportunity to make any of those decisions you refer to. It was partly my fault. I should have put my foot down years ago. It just seemed easier to let him handle the finances of the household. Now it's coming back to bite me in the ass."

"This place has been a bad influence on you."

"Oh, really? How so?"

"You never used to swear before."

"And I still haven't. Believe me, you'll know when I swear."

"And that woman—the one in the wheelchair—can't you see she has the hots for you?"

"The hots?"

"She's trying to seduce you."

"Get a grip!" Doris's voice rose in volume. She took a deep breath and let it out slowly. "You're trying to side-track me and I won't have it. You stole from me. You are also profiting from me."

"Now what are you talking about?"

"I'm referring to the matter of you living in my house and renting out your own. Care to explain?"

"I'm using the opportunity to get some money together to pay back the loan."

"Why didn't you just rent out my house?"

"I could get more for my house."

"So you're going to use money that should be mine in rent on my home to pay back a loan that was also my money. Where does your money come into it?"

"You can just as easily call the loan null and void," Sandra said.

"In what part of the legal code does it say that an unpaid loan is null and void?"

"When it's classed as a gift." Sandra glared at her. "So, it's come down to money. I thought blood was thicker than water, or money for that matter."

"You are accusing me of thinking about money first? That's rather hypocritical of you, don't you think?"

"Mother, why am I here?"

"I had hoped for some sort of explanation that I could accept. So far, I haven't heard anything remotely repentant. Can you at least tell me why you had a change of heart for me coming here?"

"Does it really matter?"

"Of course it matters. Can't you tell me the truth just this once?"

"Fine. I thought if you moved out of the house you would find out about the bank. Retirement places require bonds and such. I thought you would check your records."

"That makes sense. What changed your mind?"

"I saw this dump. When I heard about the deal you would have with them I knew you wouldn't be looking into your finances. I figured I could make some money by using your place rent-free and renting out my place."

Doris shook her head. "So you were going to give me some of your rent to cover what you thought my home was worth then pocket the rest."

"Do you want me to say I'm sorry? All right, I'm sorry."

It was a pitiful apology at best. "No, you're not. You think I owe you this, but I don't. This money is all I have to survive on until I die and you are intent on taking it away from me. In my book, that's unforgivable."

"Fine. If you want to ignore what daddy wanted you're on your own."

"Is that your final answer?" Doris looked at the woman she thought she knew.

"Until you acknowledge all the things that daddy and I have done for you, yes. I won't be coming back. You know how to contact me if you change your mind."

"Right." Doris felt her anger rise. "This is what's going to happen. I want you out of my house by the end of the week. Your guardian status of my bank account has been revoked and I will be changing my will as soon as possible. The two hundred and fifty thousand dollars you stole is your legacy, Sandra. You'll get no more from me, including the house. Your greed has cost you your inheritance."

Sandra stood and leaned on the table "I'll fight it."

Doris stared her right in the eye. "Try it."

Sandra gathered her bag and walked out of the house, slamming the front door as she left.

Phyllis moved into the room a moment later. "Everything okay?"

Doris slumped back in her chair. "No, it's not okay."

Phyllis rolled her wheelchair closer until she was next to her. She reached out her hand. Doris looked at it with tear-filled eyes before taking it in her own a moment later. "Thanks." She sniffed and a tissue appeared in front of her. "Thanks," she said again. After she blew her nose she asked, "How much did you hear?"

"Everything."

"Was I right? Maybe I overreacted."

"If it were me, I would have smacked her upside the head for talking to me like that." Phyllis squeezed her hand. "You said what you believed, now stay strong."

"I won't get to see the grandkids."

"How often do you see them now?"

Doris hesitated, as if she was trying to remember. "Umm."

"Enough said. What's Sandra's husband like?"

"Garth? I always liked him."

"Do you think he feels the same way as Sandra?"

Doris contemplated the question. "I don't know. I don't think so. He's always been polite."

"Then maybe you can work around Sandra and arrange letters, or visits, with Garth when Sandra's not around."

"That's sneaky. I don't know—"

"Do you want to see those kids or not?"

"Of course, what sort of question is that?"

"Sandra's not playing fair. Why should you?"

"Because I don't want to become her, Phyll."

Phyllis smiled at the use of the diminutive of her name. It sounded cute coming from Doris's mouth, but from the others it was just plain annoying. "If you play fair, you'll miss out. It's that simple."

"I don't know…"

"Think of it as part of your new outlook on life. You've finally grown a pair and now it's time to use 'em."

"A pair of what? Are you speaking English?"

Phyllis sighed and shook her head, her clasped hand dropping to her lap. "Doris. Doris. Doris. You have to keep up with the lingo. A pair of balls. Finding your courage. I can see you have a lot to learn."

"And you're going to teach me?"

Phyllis rubbed her hands together. "That could be dangerous."

"But will you?"

Phyllis's lips spread into an indulgent smile. "Of course I will."

"What should I do?"

"You sh—. You're doing it again. It's your decision."
"That's the problem."

Chapter Twenty-five

An Unexpected Ally

"Can I come in?"

"Please do."

"Grandma!" The two boys threw their arms around Doris's waist and hugged her tightly. She returned the hug with as much strength as she could muster. It seemed she hadn't lost her family just yet.

"What a surprise!" she gushed. Doris looked over the heads of her grandchildren to their father and saw concern there. "Caitlin!" Doris waved the young woman toward her and made the introductions. "This is my son-in-law, Garth, and his two boys, Alex and Simon. This is Caitlin. She runs the home and looks after us."

"Pleased to meet you." Garth sounded genuinely happy to meet her. It was a far cry from her daughter's reaction.

"How about we see what I can offer you two boys. I'm sure I can come up with some milk and cookies. Does that sound okay?"

The boys looked at their father and he nodded in approval before they followed Caitlin to the kitchen.

"I'm surprised to see you," Doris said in a low tone.

"I didn't know whether you'd want to see me."

"She told you?"

"Yeah."

The conversation stopped when the boys returned with their goodies. Caitlin had already put on the kettle for her never-ending supply of coffee and the conversation was kept light and polite through the afternoon tea.

Doris was itching to talk to Garth but the kids hovered around her like bees to honey. She felt Caitlin's gaze on her.

191

"I tell you what, boys. We've just got some new board games. How about we try one out?"

"What have you got?" The older boy, Alex, followed her pointing finger to the sideboard where the games were stacked. "Can we play this one?"

"Sure we can." Caitlin glanced at Doris and titled her head toward the back door.

"Thank you," Doris mouthed and was given a smile in return. "Come on." She stood and waited for Garth to do the same, before she led him out to the back patio. "Have a seat." Doris claimed the seat nearest the door while Garth took the one next to her. She waited for him to compose himself.

"It's a real mess."

"I know. What did she tell you?" Doris suspected that Garth's view would not be the same as hers.

"That you're kicking us out of your house and the money you gave her you want back."

"Why are you here?"

"To hear the truth."

Doris stared at him, not believing what she had just heard. "You don't believe her?"

He sighed and looked out over the backyard. "I suppose it's my own fault. I let things get out of hand." Doris's laugh drew his attention. "What's so funny?"

The back screen door squeaked as it opened. Phyllis pushed her wheelchair out and deposited a jug of water and two glasses on the small bench beside the chairs. "Caitlin didn't want you two to get too dehydrated out here." She hesitated. "I'm assuming you're Garth. Can I say something here?"

"Well, errr..."

"Phyllis knows all about it." Doris nodded.

"You two are more alike than you know. You both have a partner who has dominated you to the point of making your decisions for you." When Garth's eyebrow rose, Phyllis continued, "I heard your last comment. They got so used to being in charge that they felt you owed them something. Garth, Sandra tried to claim money that she had no right to. She stole it."

"Stole? Sandra?"

"Inheritances bring out the worst in people. Now, Doris here would smooth these facts to try and protect you both. That's just who she is. But I have no qualms about revealing her duplicity."

When Doris laughed Phyllis ducked her head. "Yeah, I know, I used a big word."

"Why on earth would she do that? I don't understand."

"Some months ago she asked Doris to put her house up as collateral on a loan. What was the loan for?"

"What loan?"

"Why does that not surprise me? You didn't suddenly have extra money?"

"Sandra said something about a bonus from work. How big was this loan that required you to put up the house?"

"Two hundred thousand dollars."

"Two hun—. You have got to be kidding me."

"Sandra said that you were in dire straits. It was about three months after Norman died."

"Was it around the time of the reading of the will?" Phyllis asked.

"Not long after. How did you know?"

"It all seems to tie in. I think your husband said something to make Sandra believe he was leaving her a sum of money when he died. When she didn't get it, she tried to obtain what she thought was promised to her unethically, if not, illegally."

"That's no excuse—"

"No, but do you think your talk with her put the matter to rest?" When no answer came, Phyllis made her excuses. "Yeah, well, I'll leave you two to it. Sorry for barging in."

"Phyllis—"

"No, it's none of my business. We'll try to keep the kids occupied until you're ready."

Doris felt the ache emanating from Phyllis from where she was seated. She was hurt and they both knew it. Doris waited until the back door closed before she continued.

"Is she right?" Garth asked.

"She's pretty smart." A smile accompanied the statement. "I think Phyllis didn't want us to waste time dancing around the issue."

"So, what do I do?"

"Water?" Doris used the time to think of an answer. "I really don't know," she said as she handed him a glass of water before taking one for herself.

"Do you have evidence of this… theft?" He grimaced after he said the word.

"I do, but I don't want to use it. She's still my child, Garth, and as a mother I want to protect my child."

"She probably knows that. I think the problem is that both of us are unwilling to resort to blackmail. If she's capable of stealing money from her own mother I don't think blackmail would be a problem for her."

"Where did I go wrong?" Doris ran her finger across the frosted glass, drawing a line in the condensation.

"What did you say to her?"

"I told her to get out of my house—that part is true—because she was planning to use the rent from your house to pay off the loan."

"That seems reasonable, doesn't it?"

"It would be if she was paying rent on my house, but she isn't. She moved in without my knowledge, Garth. She was living in a house, rent-free, while she made money on your house. No money was coming out of her pocket. Effectively, she was paying back the loan with my money." Doris couldn't tell whether Garth got the point or not, and she was not sure about it herself. The only thing she knew was that her daughter had turned out to be cold and heartless and she had done nothing to stop it happening. There was a lot of guilt involved in the matter.

"What I don't get is why the extra money she stole out of your account."

"Two hundred and fifty thousand dollars."

"That's nearly half a million in total!" Garth gulped down the water. "Holy hell! What was she thinking!"

"She told me it was to pay off the initial loan to save my house."

"That's something, surely—"

"She shouldn't have been in that position to start with, Garth!" Doris's voice rose in anger. "She's using the money to pay off a loan for money in her possession. I'm paying two hundred and fifty thousand for a house I already own. It doesn't take a rocket scientist to realize this is wrong."

"Which brings us back to the initial question. What do we do about it?"

"Short of turning her in to the police, I don't know."

"Would your friend have any ideas?"

"Phyllis? Maybe." Doris stood up and stretched, her bones audibly creaking from the movement. She opened the back door. "Phyllis? Can you come here a moment?"

The slight squeak of wheels announced Phyllis's approach. "Yeah?" she asked cautiously.

"We'd like to ask you a question or two. Are you up to it?"

"Sure." She waited for Doris to stand aside before moving the chair through the door. "What's up?"

"Have you got any ideas about Sandra?"

"What are you prepared to do?"

"Do?" Garth looked from Phyllis to Doris.

"How far are you going to go to stop her?"

"I just want to know what's going on."

"And you?" Phyllis asked Doris. "Do you feel the same?"

"On the one hand I just want it to all go away, but does that make me as guilty as her by not doing anything about it?"

"If you don't do anything about it she's going to think she can do anything she wants. There will be no consequences for her actions," Phyllis said gravely. "Without getting the cops involved, you may have to get your hands a little dirty."

"How dirty?"

"A bit of fact collecting may be involved."

"You mean blackmail."

"Blackmail is such an ugly word. It's more an insurance policy. If she thinks you two know about her dealings she may just want to do something about it."

"Sandra would never harm us."

"You believed Sandra would never steal either. She proved you wrong on that point." Phyllis said. "I think you need to know what she wanted the money for."

"What do you want us to do?" Garth asked with resignation.

"Doris, you stay away from Sandra. Let her think the matter is settled. Garth, you'll need to be a little more proactive. We need to get into your house and search for any sort of paperwork involving a large amount of cash."

"Can't I do that myself?"

"Your job is to keep her out of the house. It would probably be better if she didn't know you were involved; that you're still as much in the dark as you ever were. Do you want her to catch you going through her personal papers? It could get ugly." Garth winced. "Sorry to be blunt, but there should be someone 'on the inside' who may pick up on a relevant conversation or two."

"You should have become a private investigator."

"Nah, I don't have the patience for it. Besides, my hip won't allow me to go climbing in windows."

"Who do you have in mind for the break-in?" Phyllis smiled, and Doris knew who she was thinking of. "Oh no, anyone but her. Please."

"Who are you talking about?"

"Alice would be perfect, and you know it."

"Who's Alice?"

"She's an eighty year-old woman with dementia."

"She's a *sprightly* eighty year-old woman who has the energy of a fourteen year-old and can out-think the rest of us."

"Eighty?! She'd break a hip getting up our stairs."

"You haven't met Alice, have you?"

"No please, Phyllis. Let the poor man be."

"Unless you want to get Caitlin or the doc involved, it's Alice or nothing."

"This is getting messier by the moment."

"Is she going to steal the papers?" Garth sounded panicky.

"Maybe the doc can lend us her cell and Alice can take photos."

"Isn't that a little complicated for her?"

"Doris, the woman counts cards. How hard can it be?"

"No good comes from the saying 'how hard can it be'. Are you going to tell Caitlin?"

"I think she needs to know."

Doris sighed. It seemed the wheels were in motion and unless she was prepared to throw herself under the wagon the decision had been made.

Chapter Twenty-six

Undercover Blues

Alice stood at the front door with the key left by Garth. She couldn't stop a smile cross her lips. The operation came from the major herself. Take photos of the Top Secret papers and get the hell out. She could handle that. In fact, she relished the idea of finally contributing to the war effort.

She glanced around one final time before slipping the key into the lock. The satisfying click as the key turned started Alice's senses a tingling. This was her destiny, to go down in the Annals of resistance fighting as the savior of freedom.

Alice followed the instructions of the spy to where he thought the papers might be. The stairs looked high and imposing and it took more effort than she thought possible to negotiate them. Why did the enemy feel it necessary to store important papers on the top floor? Maybe her own response was why. It took too much damn energy to get there.

She stopped at the top of the staircase and leaned heavily against the wall. It took all her strength to stop herself from falling down. Maybe she could rest for a short while before continuing. What did the spy say? Maybe three hours? He was wining and dining the enemy while she took the photos.

The sight of an empty bed was almost too much. A few minutes. That's all she needed. Just a few minutes.

Alice reclined on what she assumed was a child's bed, but it was too soft for her aging back. Suddenly she felt she had stepped into a storybook. "Stop it now. Remember the mission." But Alice's body was already seeking sleep.

Finally she found the main bedroom. Another bed. Why did this building have so many beds? Alice shook her head to dispel the lethargy creeping over her. Where would that viper hide her papers? As her first choice, she poked around the most obvious drawers. With disgust she pulled out some lingerie. "The hussy," she muttered. But it didn't stop her taking a photo or two with the camera the major had supplied.

She didn't get why a telephone had a camera in it. That's what cameras were for, wasn't it? A telephone was for conversation and a camera was for photos. None of this crossing functionality lines, so she was glad when the major didn't give her the phone, instead substituting a camera. Now, that she could understand.

Alice used the camera with impunity, taking photos of anything that took her fancy. She finally remembered what she was there for and continued her search. At the back of the closet, tucked away under some blankets, was a large petty cash tin. Now this was more like a place for hiding secrets.

Alice returned to the double bed and sat down, placing the box on the duvet. It was locked. Instead of frustrating her it made Alice smile. She reached into her hair and pulled out a pin. It had been a while but like most things she never forgot the secret of lock-picking.

It took just under two minutes to open the box but Alice didn't mind the delay. Patience was something she had learned as a child, even if adulthood was littered with pockets of vagueness. She had sometimes taken those missing moments as a blessing because she'd never know what things she had done, good or bad. Every day was like starting anew; a new page to write her life upon.

Alice rummaged through the papers inside. "Look for papers with large amounts of money," the major had said. There weren't a lot of documents so she decided to take pictures of them all. She moved the papers to the bathroom where she could get good light for the photo. One by one she snapped them. She didn't bother to see whether it was relevant or not, instead using the time to take as many snaps as she could. She had viewed the first page to make sure she had the right information. After that, she took the photos, one after the other. Boredom had set in by the fourth or fifth page and her mind started to wander. She was already looking around for something to add to the picture. Paper was plain and needed something cheerful to add color and vibrancy to the display. Before she knew it, Alice was adding a flower here or bath pearls there as decoration to each page before taking a photo.

"That's better," she whispered and smiled at her brilliant idea. Black and white was boring, even though that was the color of choice for the 1940s.

Finally, her mission was complete and she replaced the locked box in its original position. She took a moment to use the bathroom. One sad consequence she found was that her body wanted to pee at the oddest of times, and not knowing what she would face in the next couple of hours Alice was one to take advantage of the opportunity presented to her.

She had just finished washing her hands when she heard the front door open. "Oh, crud." The stairs were no longer an option. The voices became louder and she knew the family had returned. Where did the three hours go?

Alice trundled into the main bedroom and searched for a hiding place. Her most immediate choice was the closet, but her enemies were smart and often looked there first. Behind the door? That was fine until they closed the door. There seemed to be nowhere to hide. She moved toward the door to look for another room to hide in.

The voices echoed up the stairwell. She had no option but to seek refuge in the main bedroom. Frantically she searched for somewhere, her gaze resting on the huge bed in the middle of the room. *How cliché*, she thought, right before her body hit the floor and she rolled underneath it. From her place under the bed she observed two sets of feet enter the room.

"That was nice, Garth. Now, what's going on?"

"On? I thought I'd take my family out to dinner. Is that a crime?"

"Hmmm."

The female voice was tinged with scepticism, and Alice agreed. She would have been sceptical as well. Men were just too easy to read.

"You don't sound very convinced."

"I'm not. You won't go out to dinner unless I drag you by your ear. Did you get fired from your job?"

"No, of course not. It's been quite a while since we actually went out. I thought it would be nice—"

"Fine. I won't argue." The female sighed loudly. "Thank you," she said softly.

There was silence for a moment or two and Alice cringed. They were probably kissing or something. Alice stayed where she was and thought of other things while they did whatever they were doing.

Alice stayed put and waited for the man and the woman to finally get to sleep. She hadn't been aware of when she herself drifted off to sleep.

†

The strains of 'I Got You Babe' filled the silence of the car. Mel bolted upright and took a moment to get her bearings. She quickly glanced at her watch before answering the cell. "Hello?" Her voice still held the remnants of sleep.

"Doctor Stokes?" the male voice on the other end whispered.

"Yes?"

"It's Garth."

For a moment she thought he was one of her patients. "Do you know what time it is?"

"Garth… Sandra's husband."

"Oh, sorry. Where's Alice?"

"I think she's under our bed. I can hear snoring coming from there. At least, I hope it's her or we have an intruder."

"Damn it, Alice!" Mel ground out.

"I don't think I can get her out without waking Sandra. What do you want me to do?"

Things had gone to hell, just as she thought they would. "Leave her be. We'll have to try to get her out in the morning. If you get the chance, tell her to wait." Having Alice in the house was asking for trouble but there was nothing she could do short of bashing on the front door. "Thanks, Garth."

He grunted and the phone went dead. Mel's head fell back against the headrest of her seat. Caitlin obviously wasn't worried about the mission because Mel hadn't heard from her since she picked up Alice. Maybe it was time to call her.

"Hello?" Caitlin's voice was sleep-tainted.

"I thought you would have been calling every five minutes by now."

"Mel?"

"No, it's KIKK FM asking you for the answer to who our mystery guest is. Of course it's Mel!"

"Don't get grumpy at me. It's... one a.m. One a.m.??? Where's Alice? Has something happened?"

"You could say that. She's still inside and stuck under the double bed."

"Stuck as in unable to move?"

"Stuck, as in Sandra and Garth are asleep on top of said bed, with Alice underneath snoring quietly. Without waking Sandra, Garth can't get Alice out."

"But she is okay, right?"

"Yeah, she's fine. It looks like I'm sticking around until morning."

"I'm so sorry, Mel. It wasn't supposed to take this long."

"It can't be helped."

"What about work?"

"I'll worry about it in the morning. I'm not calling Alex at this hour. I'll call you in the morning when I have Alice. Sleep tight."

"You too."

After Caitlin hung up Mel muttered, "As well as I can on a car seat." She stepped out of the car and walked around it a couple of times to get her blood flowing. The next time they asked her for a favor she was going to run for the hills.

Chapter Twenty-Seven

Crossing the Line in the Sand

It had been a hasty few hours before she saw any sign of Alice, what with watching Garth head off to work, then Sandra taking the kids to school. She was ready to munch on her nails as Alice's non-appearance kept her on the edge of her seat. Mel had to wait until after nine a.m. before the old woman emerged, a beaming smile on her face as if she didn't have a care in the world. She, on the other hand, had to organize patient cancellations where she couldn't get Alex to cover for her. It had not been pretty and only hoped that the pictures were worth it.

"What happened?"

"They came home early." Alice climbed into the car and closed the door.

"They came home on time, Alice. You had three hours. What were you doing all that time?"

"Reconnaissance takes time, Major. This building took longer than normal, what with all the beds inside. It must have been the barracks."

"Well?"

Alice looked at her. "Well what?"

"The photos, Alice. Did you get the photos?" Mel sighed.

"Some pretty nice ones, Major."

Mel started the engine and pulled out from the curb. "Good." She drove Alice back to the home and brought in her laptop.

"Are you all right?" Caitlin asked Alice, forgetting Mel was also present. She led Alice off toward the dining room.

"I'm fine. Thanks for asking," Mel muttered then followed them.

"Here's the camera." Alice handed it to Mel, who set down her laptop and booted it up.

"Let's see what we have here." She was not going to work before seeing what all the fuss was about.

"Do you want me to get Doris?"

"How about we see what it is first before getting Doris excited."

Mel plugged the camera cord into her laptop and waited for the program to download the photos. Finally she could see shot after shot of white. She only hoped that the white had writing on it. "Okaaayyy." Mel studied the first few enlarged photos and saw they were contracts of sorts, between Sandra, someone named David Devereaux and a company called Piralis Medical. She quickly scanned all the photos, even the ones with the flowery decorations around the edges. "What are these?" she asked Alice.

"I got tired of taking black and white photos, so I thought I'd gussy it up a little."

Caitlin looked over Mel's shoulder at the photos in question. "It certainly makes looking at the documents a lot easier on the eye."

"Don't start."

"So?"

"What's going on?" Isabel entered the dining room and saw the laptop. "Oh, great! A computer. Can I see?"

"Sure. Just don't touch anything." Mel stepped aside and let Isabel sit down.

"I wonder who Piralis Medical is?"

"Want me to find out?" Isabel asked and proceeded to do a search before Mel even had the chance to open her mouth. "Let's see…" She scanned the results, clicked a few times then did another search. "It may take a little while."

"Coffee?" Caitlin asked.

Mel was worried that Isabel would wipe the computer and they'd lose the photos so she wasn't sure what to do. Before she could voice her concern Isabel handed the camera back to her.

"Just in case, the photos are still on the camera."

Mel blinked at the camera then at Isabel. The house surely had some magical property that made its residents psychic.

"Coffee!" Caitlin called from the kitchen.

Mel left Isabel to her own devices and prayed that the woman knew what she was doing. The laptop not only had her patient files on it but it was also her lifeline to what was going on in the world. If that failed she would have to use the television as a final resort. The thought of sitting through an endless array of news bulletins and breaking news spots made her cringe.

"Just for my peace of mind, can you say something other than 'coffee'? I want to know it's not my mind substituting the word for whatever you're trying to say."

"I said 'coffee' twice. Anything else was a real word."

"Thank God."

"I want to thank you for looking out for Alice. I'm sorry that it lasted all night."

"Me too. I had to re-schedule some morning appointments."

"Oh, Lord! I am so sorry."

"Stop worrying. I wanted to make sure she was fine. Besides, she could have panicked if she had been met by anyone else."

"I hope this is the end of it."

"For us, maybe, but I think it's just the beginning for Doris."

"I, ah…," Caitlin twirled her coffee cup. "Will I see you this weekend?"

"Do you want to?"

"I asked you first."

"Yes, I would love to see you this weekend, the more skin the better." Caitlin blushed and Mel dissolved into peals of laughter. "It's a little late for that."

"I know. I still can't believe I did that."

"I would hope that you mean 'I can't believe WE did that.'"

Caitlin ducked her head.

"I hate to tease and leave, but I do have a job and patients waiting. I'll call you later to see how things went." Mel stood and took the mug to the sink. Caitlin walked her to the door and opened it.

"Before you go, you may want to see this," Isabel said from her crouched position over the laptop.

"What did you find?"

"It's fake."

"Piralis?"

"Yep. Doesn't exist. Probably been set up to fool Sandra, maybe even more. There's no knowing how many victims there are for this scam."

Mel gazed at Isabel. "How the hell did you find this out so quickly?"

Isabel smiled at her and gave her a wink.

"You're not CIA or something, are you?" Mel asked.

"I could tell you but then I'd have to kill you."

"What are you going to do now?" Mel could see Caitlin shifting restlessly beside her.

"First, I'm going to have a talk with Isabel and find out exactly who is living under my roof. Then I think it's time that Doris knew the truth."

†

"What am I doing here?"

"This has got to end." Doris said.

"What has to end? Make some sense."

"Stop this nonsense. We're going to get to the bottom of this right now."

"If you say so." Sandra sat down on a dining room chair and waited.

"Well?"

"Well what?" Sandra looked at Doris benevolently. It made Doris want to smack the disinterested look off her face.

"How about we start with the original loan of two hundred thousand dollars? What did you want that for?"

"Why should I tell you? It's none of your business."

"Using my house for collateral makes it my business. Answer the question."

"I had an emergency."

"What sort of emergency needed that sort of cash? Gambling?"

"Yes," Sandra sighed, "it was a gambling debt."

"You can't help yourself, can you? We both know that's a lie."

"If you know, why are you asking me?" The look on Sandra's face was anything but comforting. It was the face of a woman who thought her secret was safe.

There was a knock at the door. "Caitlin? Could you answer that please?" Even though she was closer, Doris didn't want to give Sandra the chance to think. "You have to do better than that, my girl."

Caitlin passed them on the way to the door. She opened it and Garth stepped in. "Where are the boys?"

"They're in the car."

"Bring them in and we'll keep them occupied outside."

He quickly stepped out and returned two minutes later with his sons. Caitlin ushered them out the back door to the backyard.

"What are you doing here?"

"Doris asked me here."

Sandra looked at her mother.

"He has a right to know."

"You don't seem to get it. There is no conspiracy. The money was used to pay a gambling debt."

Doris knew what she was thinking. It was an opportunity to make Doris look like her mind was slipping, which would give her ample evidence to contest a will. But she would have none of that. She had been silent for too long and it was time to take back her dignity. "And the second amount of money?"

"To pay back the original loan from the bank. I've already told you all this."

"So you can produce paperwork to show that the money you stole from me was to pay back the bank?"

"Yes. Mother, I'm getting tired of your constant, almost paranoid, preoccupation with this money. Are you all right?"

Doris stopped herself from responding to the jibe and glared at her. "Piralis Medical." She took a small amount of satisfaction from seeing Sandra's face blanch. "Care to explain?"

"Garth, can you get us some coffee?" Sandra asked

"Garth, stay put. You need to hear this."

"I've never heard that name before."

"Funny, it was found on documents with your name on it. I would have assumed that you would have read any paperwork before signing it."

"I could have you arrested for breaking and entering."

"That's rich coming from you," Doris growled.

"It's not breaking and entering when they were invited in," Garth said quietly. Sandra glared at him with something akin to hostility.

"Traitor!" she hissed.

"If you had told me what was going on…"

"You didn't need to know."

"I'm your husband!" he yelled. "Of course, I needed to know!" He dropped to one knee in front of Sandra. "What could be so bad that you had to lie, cheat and steal for it? Did you think I would leave?"

"What do you care? You were always at work. I was the one who had to run this family. You didn't make any decisions then, and you certainly don't now!"

As Doris listened she could imagine the same words coming out of her husband's mouth. Sandra had learned well. "Stop it! Don't become your father."

"Daddy has nothing to do with this."

"Of course, he does. Don't you listen to yourself? What you just said could very well have been said by him." Doris felt the truth of it.

"Get to the point."

"All right. You want the bald truth? Here it is. You had an affair with a man named David Devereaux. Once the affair was established, he told you he was dying and that there was some sort of revolutionary medical treatment in Switzerland that could save his life. Of course, it would cost a lot of money—two hundred thousand dollars to be exact. You said, 'sure' because you had expected a windfall after your dad died. When that didn't happen, you were forced to get a bank loan to cover your promise." Doris watched Sandra's head drop. "When did you find out? After he left you or when you finally checked out who Piralis Medical was or, in this case, who they weren't."

"There's nothing illegal about me giving money to someone."

Sandra was fighting, Doris had to give her that. "No, but David did. He conned you. You overstepped the mark when you stole the money to pay back the loan then tried to cover it up."

"And when were you going to tell me, Sandra?" Garth looked at her with disillusionment. "Never?"

"Why can't you all just leave me alone?" Sandra stood and pushed Garth back onto his ass. She paced the room. "What do you want from me?"

"The truth, Sandra. I want to hear it from your lips."

"And what will that accomplish?"

"That you can tell the truth for once. I want some respect. All my married life I've been thought of as a second-class citizen, a moron. I was talked down to like some five year old. Just because I was never asked for an opinion didn't mean I didn't have one." Doris became agitated and it took some mental wrangling on her part to get herself under control. She didn't want the conversation to deteriorate into an all-out yelling match.

"Yes, I had an affair." Sandra glanced at Garth to see his reaction. "Yes, he conned me. Yes, I stole the money from your bank account."

"Garth?"

"I don't know what to think. It's a lot to take in."

Sandra addressed Garth, "Will you forgive me?"

"I... I don't know." Garth stood and walked out the back door.

"Why did you have to destroy my life?"

"That was not my intention. You did these things, Sandra, not me. If anyone is to blame, it's you."

"It's not me. It's... it's..." Sandra finally sat down again and slumped in her chair. "How did you find out all this?"

"The marvel of the internet, my dear. Plus a guess or two. It didn't take much to figure it out once we knew the medical place didn't exist."

"We?"

"Me and my friends here. They are very resourceful."

"So, everyone knows?"

"No, only those who matter to me. As to who else depends on you. I have no inclination to see you in jail, but that could change if you cause any more trouble. Do I make myself clear?"

"And Garth?"

"That's your problem, not mine. Now go home and start to mend those bridges."

Sandra stood and walked to the back door. "Garth! Kids! Time to go home!" She turned and regarded her mother. "I didn't think you had it in you." Sandra's lips curled slightly upward. "I think daddy may have been wrong."

"He was." Doris stood and waited for her family to assemble and head to the front door. "Oh, and Sandra? I expect to see you and your family at least once a month. Is that understood?"

"Yes, Mother."

"Goodbye, kids."

"Bye, grandma!"

Doris gave Garth a sympathetic nod as he left behind his family. The door finally closed on a traumatic episode in Doris's life.

"Are you okay?" Phyllis's familiar presence filled the doorway.

"I think so. I hope so."

"You did a brave thing," she said as she moved the wheelchair into the room.

"Somehow having you nearby made me think it was okay to say what I did. Do you think it'll make a difference?"

"I think so. More than the last time. I don't know if having Garth there changed everything, or whether she finally realized you were a human being."

Doris smiled. "You make me sound so appealing."

"It'll all work out. You'll see." Phyllis leaned back in her chair and rested her arms on the armrests.

"I hope so. How could she be so stupid?"

"Don't go there. It's not your problem. It's something that Sandra, and Garth, will have to work out. However, I have to say that if she fell into the affair there must have been some concerns even then. She wouldn't have succumbed so easily if she was happy."

Doris grinned.

"Yeah, I know," she whispered, "I used another big word." Phyllis tilted her head to one side and regarded a despondent Doris. "Do you feel up to a walk?"

"Sure. I'll be back in a minute." Phyllis's gaze followed Doris as she walked down the hallway.

"Never thought I'd see you like this."

Phyllis couldn't work up the effort to make a pithy comment to Sophie. "Hmmm."

"It might be a lost cause."

"It's not about sex, Soph." Phyllis said as her gaze remained on the hallway. "I know what the stakes are."

"And you'd be happy with that?"

Phyllis turned her attention to her friend leaning on the back of a chair. "Yeah, I would. She's a nice lady. I'm content to be her friend."

"Is that how it works at this age?"

"Who knows? It's unknown territory to me."

Phyllis didn't notice Doris's return. "Me, too," Doris replied.

How much had she heard? Instead, Phyllis smiled and said, "Hello… friend. Now let's go take that walk."

†

Monday morning came around and there was peace, of sorts, in the household. Phyllis saw to Doris's anxiety by trying to keep her mind off the previous day's events. Caitlin heard Doris's nervous titter when Phyllis told some ribald joke at the dining room table. The other women had already heard that particular joke and their response was less than enthusiastic.

"Oh, come on. It's funny." Phyllis complained.

"The first three times it was funny," Isabel explained. "The last fifteen times is boring."

"Doris hasn't heard it."

"Now she has. Drop it."

A knock at the door drew their attention.

"I've got it!" Caitlin called.

She opened the door and found a stranger standing there. "Can I help you?"

The woman, in her forties and dressed in a crisp blue suit, smiled at her. "Are you…," she consulted her clip board, "Caitlin Joseph?"

"Yes I am." Caitlin started to sweat. Was this going to cost her dearly? She already had enough trials in her life, so she didn't need one more.

"My name is Alison Burgess and I'm from Sole Care. We are a charitable organization whose aim is to help the elderly. A concerned citizen informed us that you were a worthy cause in need of our help."

Caitlin knew exactly who the concerned citizen was, and she was going to have a stern word with her. "I don't need your help."

"Please, don't take this as a slight on your care for these women. We only want to give you some assistance to make things easier for you."

Caitlin eyed her suspiciously. "What sort of help?"

"We have a painter who has offered to give the outside of the house a new coat, plus a local hardware store is willing to donate the paint."

Caitlin could live with that. She had always been unhappy that she couldn't present a nicer image to the outside world, but it was something that she knew she could never afford to do. "That's it?"

"We also have a volunteer who is prepared to come in one afternoon a week to help out. I know it's not much—"

"No! No. It's just right."

Alison smiled. "Good to hear. Now I just have some paperwork that needs to be filled out and we can get onto this right away."

"Come in." Caitlin stood aside and let Alison enter. She introduced her to her charges then found a seat at the table for her.

It looked like things were looking up. There was a little spare cash in the account. The house would get a makeover. She finally had a love life. And she would soon have one afternoon a week off to recuperate. It just didn't get better than this.

She then asked the inevitable question, "Coffee?"

About the Author

Erica Lawson

Erica Lawson is a "dinky di" Aussie, born and raised in Sydney, Australia, 57 years ago. She has worked as a secretary for most of her working life in a variety of interesting fields from a government scientific organization, the fire brigade, the film industry and finally, for the last 20 years, with a psychiatrist. Many of her friends will attest to the fact that she finally found her niche in the last job, gaining many helpful hints for her own state of mind.

Her first book, "Possessing Morgan", was released in December 2009. It is a winner of the 2010 GCLS award for best thriller/mystery novel. Her second book "The Chronicles of Ratha: The Children Of The Noorthi", a science fiction adventure, was released in December 2010 and a finalist in the 2012 GCLS Awards. Erica's third novel, "Soulwalker" was released in February 2012, a Rainbow Award winner for Best Science-Fiction story of 2012, and a 2013 GCLS Finalist.

She has two new releases. "Miss-Match" (co-authored with A.C. Henley) is due out in April 2013 through Affinity eBooks, Amazon and Barnes and Noble.

The second book, "Reflected Passion" is due out some time May/June 2013 through Blue Feather Books, Amazon and normal retail outlets.

Erica Lawson also writes under the name "Aurelia" on online fan fiction.

Other Books from Affinity

Beginning of the End—**Alane Hotchkin** What happens when life doesn't go exactly as you planned and you must protect others from your own fate? Escaping a horrific childhood, Nikki longed to find happily ever after in adulthood. What she found was Hell. Or did it find her? Finding the courage to break the cycle of betrayal, she opens her heart one last time. Alex lived a childhood others dreamed of. Her father never once denied the young rebel a thing. All her life she dreamed of protecting others; to follow in her father's footsteps. Soon though she learned sex and fists made the most powerful of weapons. Alex controls the women in her life through fear and sex, will breaking the cycle be too much to overcome? Will loving Nikki be enough to change her, or is Alex beyond help?

Alex would give Nikki the world, but at what price? When a person's tightly controlled reality snaps, what then…? This is the Beginning of the End for one of them and the ultimate sacrifice for the other. But who is who in this game of life?

Galveston 1900: Swept Away—**Linda Crist** On September 7-8, 1900, the island of Galveston, Texas, was destroyed by a hurricane, or 'tropical cyclone' as it was called in those days. This story is a fictional account of Mattie and Rachel, two women who lived there, and their lives during the time of the 'great storm'. Forced to flee from her family at a young age, Rachel Travis finds a home and livelihood on the island of Galveston. Independent, friendly, and yet often lonely, only one other person knows the dark secret that haunts her. Madeline "Mattie" Crockett is trapped in a loveless marriage, convinced that her fate is sealed. She never dares to dream of true happiness, until Rachel Travis comes walking into her life. As emotions come to light, the storm of Mattie's marriage converges with the very real hurricane. Can they survive, and build the life they both dream of?

This second edition of one of Linda Crist's best-loved novels maintains the original story, while incorporating some reader-pleasing passages that were cut from the first edition. As an added bonus, the short story "Something to Celebrate" is included at the end of the novel, detailing further adventures of Rachel and Mattie.

Rapture: Sins of the Sinners—A. C. Henley & Fran Heckrotte A serial killer is targeting young lesbians throughout the state of Texas. Texas Ranger Cochetta Lovejoy is assigned to the case. Convinced she knows who is committing the murders, Ranger Lovejoy is willing to do whatever it takes to put the perpetrator behind bars--even if it means stretching the limits of the law by manipulating the judicial system. Detective Agnes Kelly-Elliott is one of Ft. Worth Police Department's finest investigators. When Ranger Lovejoy appears on the crime scene of a recent murder, Agnes fears a dark secret that, if revealed, could destroy her family ties and end her career. This is a dark, gritty, graphic tale of desire gone awry, and flawed characters looking for redemption in all the wrong places.

Till There Was You—S. Anne Gardner Julia is a woman used to power and is not afraid to use it or impose her will to get her way. She appears to have the world but a part of her is empty and cold as a frozen tundra. Julia rides in the mornings to clear her head and to make plans for what she is about to set in motion. Theodora, known as Teddy, is trying to put together a marriage filled with uncertainties. She felt once upon a time that she would have a great love but that has eluded her. One morning these two women meet and from the first instance, it is explosive. The attraction is undeniable, the fears very real and the end without question will change them both forever.

Denial—**Jackie Kennedy** Time spent in Somalia has Doctor Celeste Cameron accustomed to living and working in a war zone. Coming back home to America, Celeste is glad to see the end of the peril she has been in—or so she thinks. Danger seems to follow Celeste and she finds it in the shape of Amy. What Celeste feels for Amy scares her more than anything she has faced in war zones. Amy has the same feelings, but is in denial and vows to marry Josh, Celeste's twin brother, no matter what. When fate brings them together again, will they give in to their mutual attraction or will they once again deny what they feel?.

In Name Only—JM Dragon—<u>Sequel to The Fix-it Girl</u> Can an agreement forged out of necessity actually work?

'55 Ford—**Erin O'Reilly** Andrea McBride, the author of four books, wants to find someone to restore an old '55 Ford truck that she inherited in a real estate purchase. She will only settle for the best and finds RJ Whittaker who many proclaim to be the best restorer among millions.

An Affair of Love—S. Anne Gardner From a dark past, a forbidden love, a secret comes. Among the confusion and the chaos of an unwanted reality, two women find something they neither want nor can deny.

Desert Heat—**Dannie Marsden** For Luce Diamond, an undercover policewoman, her life is in shambles. Her longtime lover left her and an automobile accident that resulted in a child's death haunts her.

Taming the Wolff—**Del Robertson** ONLY ONE WOMAN...HAS THE POWER...TO TAME THE WOLFF...

Private Dancer—**TJ Vertigo** Reece Corbett grew up on the mean streets on New York City, abused, used and in trouble with the law. Faith Ashford grew up wealthy, with all the creature comforts that money provides. When they meet fireworks begin.

Miriam and Esther—**Sherry Barker** Miriam thought her life would play out in the bustling metropolis of Dallas, but after a life-changing accident, she moves to the small town of Cool Lake, Texas to get her head on straight and regain her senses.

McKee—**A.C. Henley** Private Investigator Quinlan McKee has returned to Los Angeles after a three-year absence, only to find herself embroiled in a world of child slavery and police corruption.

Bailey's Run—**Ali Spooner** Bailey Chambers mourns the loss of her lover, Nessa, in an unsolved carjacking. When Tommy, Bailey's brother becomes a victim of a gay bashing, Bailey assumes his case will be handled the same way as her lover's—lackadaisically.

Desi Dexter assigned to Tommy's case, feels Bailey's disdain toward her and her partner. Through tenacious police work, Desi, is able to uncover the reason for Bailey's attitude, and convinces her that she is sincere in solving the case.

Mutual attraction sparks, and before they can move forward with their fledging romance, Desi, and her partner Braxton, uncover the presence of a serial killer.

What will happen to Bailey, when, Desi becomes engrossed in another case? Can their relationship survive?

E-Books, Print, Free e-books
Visit our website for more publications available online.

www.affinityebooks.com

Affinity E-Book Press NZ LTD

Canterbury, New Zealand

Registered Company 2517228

www.ingramcontent.com/pod-product-compliance
Lightning Source LLC
Chambersburg PA
CBHW070109260626
47160CB00004B/1386